Books by Bill Kincaid
[All are available on Amazon & Kindle]

Ventryvian Legacy
[Science Fiction/Fantasy]

Wizard's Gambit
Kings and Vagabonds

Historical Fiction

Nicodemus' Quest
Saul's Quest
Joseph's Quest
The Making of the President:
The Nightmare Scenario

Humor/Fractured Fairy Tale

Ronald Raygun and the Sweeping Beauty

Drama/Plays

Sweeping Beauty [comedy]
Celestial Court [Christian]

Joseph's Quest

Overcoming the Obstacles and Challenges of Life

Bill Kincaid

Although *Joseph's Quest* is a work of fiction, most of the characters existed and the scenes depicted have been reconstructed as accurately as possible from data available to the author at the time the book was written. Various modern translations of the *Bible* have been used as a basis for the scenes and dialogue, although additional dialogue has been invented from the author's imagination in order to make the scenes flow more smoothly.

Copyright © 2022 by Bill Kincaid. All rights reserved. Printed in the United States of America. No part of this book may be used or reproduced in any manner whatsoever without express written permission except for brief quotations embodied in critical articles and reviews.

This book is dedicated to

Hazel Freeman,

a young lady who has impressed

her grandparents with her

love for books and reading

Forward

Joseph's Quest begins with Joseph being down in a pit. You and I might never be thrown into an empty cistern by jealous siblings—but we all have to deal with the obstacles and challenges of life. What pit are you facing? Which ones have you overcome?

Maybe you were abused as a child or were betrayed by a friend or family member. Or you may have lost your job or were diagnosed as having a life-threatening disease. The financial empire you built may have crumbled. You may now be unemployed, destitute and homeless. The love of your life may have left you or died. You may have been convicted of a crime you didn't commit. Your reputation may be tattered and ruined.

Not sure where to turn? Could you use a role model? Perhaps someone who has been down in the pits of life before successfully finding a way out could serve as a guide. It's not easy. It's not painless. But it can be done.

That's what this book is about.

We first meet Joseph in the 30th chapter of Genesis when he is born into a dysfunctional family. Although his father Jacob had children by four different women, Joseph was the first to be born to Rachel, Jacob's favorite wife. By the 37th chapter of Genesis, Joseph had grown to be a spoiled seventeen-year-old brat his older brothers couldn't stand, which is why they cast him into an abandoned cistern. They considered killing him but decided to sell him into slavery instead.

Being a slave in a foreign country where the people speak a language you don't understand has to rate as a monumental pit by anyone's standards. But it got even worse for Joseph before it got better. He could have had his own private pity party. Spoiled brats are known to do that sort of thing. He could have given up. Or let anger consume him. He could have blamed God for his troubles and mistreatment.

But instead of becoming bitter, he became better. Joseph let God teach him the lessons he needed to learn to grow into the man God could use to save his own people as well as his adopted nation.

Perhaps his true story can serve as an example for us as we struggle with the pits that obstruct our own journey along the highways and byways of life. What might we learn if we follow Joseph along the Road to Recovery?

Introduction

Pain shot through Jacob's head as he opened his eyes in the predawn darkness. His splitting headache was probably a result of drinking too much the night before. But he reasoned that it was worth it to celebrate obtaining his reward. Because he had had no money or other property to present as a dowry for the woman he loved, Jacob had spent the past seven years working for Laban, the girl's father and Jacob's uncle. Now Laban was also Jacob's father-in-law.

"Ah, Rachel, Rachel, I love you," Jacob muttered as he squeezed the sleeping woman lying next to him. *So, this is what it feels like to be married. Well, it sure beats the long, lonely nights I've spent dreaming about it!*

Jacob leaned back on the bed and closed his eyes. *A bit more sleep might help this headache go away.* When he opened his eyes in the early morning light, Jacob cuddled up again with his new wife—and sensed that something was wrong. Her hair was courser than he remembered, and it smelled more like sage than lilacs. He turned her so that she faced him—and discovered that the woman he had slept with was not Rachel but was rather her older sister.

"Leah!" he exclaimed, startled. "Why are you here?"

"Don't you remember?" she asked while holding her arms toward him, inviting his caress. "You married me last night."

"No! I worked seven years for Rachel."

"Well, you got me instead."

"We'll see about that," Jacob said while jumping out of bed and grabbing his robe. He stormed into Laban's presence and demanded, "What have you done to me? I served you faithfully for seven years with the express understanding that I would get Rachel as my wife. Why have you deceived me?"

Laban replied, "It's not our custom here to give the younger daughter in marriage before her older sister has been married. Finish this daughter's bridal week. Then I will allow you to have Rachel as well—in return for another seven years of work."

"That was not the terms of our agreement!"

"Those are the terms now—if you want Rachel as your wife. And you can have her in another week if you agree."

Thus it was that Jacob married both of Laban's daughters. Although Jacob loved Rachel more than Leah, Rachel remained barren while Leah bore him six sons and a daughter. Jacob also had two sons by Rachel's maidservant, Bilhah, and two by Leah's maidservant, Zilpah. Finally—after those ten sons and a daughter had been born—Rachel became pregnant and gave birth to a son she named Joseph, whom Jacob favored because the boy was the product of his love for Rachel.

Joseph's Quest

Overcoming the Obstacles and Challenges of Life

Chapter 1

Joseph lay at the bottom of a deep dark pit. The only light came from limited sunlight shining through a narrow opening high overhead. That wasn't much, but it allowed him to survey his dismal surroundings.

His head and left shoulder hurt from where they had collided with rocks on his way down. Blood oozed from a gash in his left arm. His voice was hoarse from screaming for help. But mostly he was shocked, dazed and scared.

He had initially been upset, angry and incredulous that his own brothers would even think of attacking him. *How dare they do such a thing? Boy, will they ever catch it when Dad finds out! I can't wait to tell him. He'll fix them. Revenge will be sweet!*

But as he considered his fate and his limited options, fear replaced disbelief, though the desire for revenge and the shock of it all remained in full force. *Throwing me into this pit is a serious enough offense they might think they can't afford to let Dad find out. What if they just leave me here—or worse. They could kill me. No one would ever know. Dad didn't know they had left Shechem and come up here to Dothan.*

Joseph's brothers had stripped him of the ornamented tunic he had been wearing, leaving him almost naked when they threw him into the pit. "Stupid!" Joseph muttered to himself. *It was stupid of me to wear that tunic. I knew they were jealous of me for being Dad's favorite son — and wearing that multicolored coat just emphasized to them that I get preferential treatment.*

From where he lay at the bottom of the abandoned cistern, Joseph could hear his brothers talking as they ate. "What should we do with dreamer boy?" one of them asked. Joseph perked up to hear their words better.

"Reuben said for us not to shed his blood," someone else answered. The voice might have been Judah's, but Joseph wasn't sure.

"Yeah, but Reuben's not here now.

What if the kid gets out of the pit and snitches on us again?"

Ah, that sounds like Dan.

"He won't get out," another said. "Simeon tied up his hands real good."

"I agree. Simeon's knots hold."

"But we're talking about Joseph. He might dream up some way of getting out."

"Ha! Dreams!" a brother laughed. "That's what helped put him in that pit."

"Let's see how well his dreams turn out if he dies down there."

Joseph drew in a quick breath. *That was another stupid thing I did. Actually, several stupid things if you count the various times I boasted to my brothers about my dreams of their bowing down to me. Did I really think they would be positively impressed by being told such things? Dumb!*

"Listen, guys. I've got a great idea."

"What is it, Judah?"

"What do we gain by killing our brother and covering up his blood? After all, he is our brother, our own flesh."

"Yeah—but what do you have in mind?"

"Do you see that caravan coming this way? It's probably Ishmaelites headed to Egypt. Come, let's sell him to the Ishmaelites. That way we make money, and we don't do away with him ourselves."

"Yeah. His blood won't be on our hands, and we also get paid."

The sounds of the caravan got louder, and then new voices and accents were added to the mix. When Joseph looked up, he saw a circle of strange faces looking down at him from the top of the cistern.

My brothers really and truly are trying to sell me as a slave to these foreigners. That's insane! That's detestable! That's ... That's ... That's ... probably better than the other option I heard them discussing. It's obvious they won't let me go free for fear of what I'll tell Dad. Being a slave will at least keep me alive with a chance to escape at some point. Then I can plot my revenge for what they've done to me.

"God, help me; give me wisdom, guidance and protection; and please stay with me," Joseph prayed as he saw Judah being lowered into the pit on a rope. Judah wrapped both the end of the rope and his own arms around Joseph, signaled to their brothers, and both men were lifted out of the pit.

"Well, here he is," Levi said to the Ishmaelites. "As you can see, he's a strong and healthy lad of seventeen years. He can work all day."

The Ishmaelites examined Joseph from head to toe, checked his teeth, and felt of his muscles. Then they huddled and discussed him in a language Joseph couldn't understand. Finally one of them turned to the brothers and said, "We'll give you ten pieces of silver for him."

"Ten?" gasped Judah. "He's worth at

least fifty. You're not going to find a better or more intelligent slave anywhere for that price."

"Don't try that line on us," said one of the traders. "You boys are desperate to get rid of him. We'll take him off your hands and pay you fifteen pieces of silver. You're in no position to bargain."

Judah looked at his brothers and mouthed a number. When they nodded, he turned and said, "Thirty."

"Twenty—and that's our last offer. Take it or we leave him with you."

Joseph's brothers looked at each other, nodded, and took the offer. The Ishmaelites counted out twenty shekels of silver, put a rope around Joseph's wrists, attached the other end of the rope to a wagon, and led him away.

The brothers killed a lamb and soaked Joseph's multicolored coat in its blood. After dirtying the tunic in the dust of the earth, they took the tunic to their father, told him they had found it lying on the ground, and asked if he recognized it.

"Oh God, no! Joseph, oh Joseph, my son, my son!" he wailed. "First my wife dies in childbirth, and now my son has been killed by a wild beast. Oh God, oh God, how could you let this happen?"

Chapter 2

The hot sun beat down on Joseph as he trudged along beside the wagon to which he was tied. He had plenty of time to think about the radical change that had suddenly happened in his life.

I knew my brothers resented me because I was Dad's favorite son, but I never imagined it would come to this: my own brothers plotting to kill me and then selling me instead to foreigners. But why? What did I do that was bad enough for them to even consider those options — much less to actually go through with it?

Joseph thought back on the words and actions of his brothers. They had questioned whether he could get out of the pit and snitch on them again. "Snitching," he muttered.

Yeah, I delighted on tattling to Dad anytime I caught them doing something wrong. I can see where they wouldn't appreciate that — especially if their kid brother was the one doing the snitching.

"Dreamer boy! What a nickname for me." Joseph spat out the words as he mentally reconstructed some of the dreams he had told his brothers. Two dreams were especially vivid in his memory. The first of them depicted the brothers binding sheaves of grain in a field when suddenly Joseph's sheaf stood up and remained upright while his brothers' sheaves gathered around it and bowed down to Joseph's sheaf.

The brothers had become angry when Joseph told them that dream—but their anger hadn't kept him from relating the second dream to them later. That vision had the sun, the moon, and eleven stars bowing down to Joseph. *Dad joined my brothers in rebuking me for that dream.* Jacob had asked, "Are we to come—your mother and I along with your brothers—and bow low to you to the ground?"

That interpretation still seemed a bit strange to Joseph, since his mother was dead at the time of the dream. Rachel had died while giving birth to the youngest brother, Benjamin. *Perhaps Dad was attempting to show how absurd the dream was so that my brothers would dismiss it rather than hating me even more for sharing it with my family. Well, if that was the case, it obviously didn't work. Those dreams hit a sore spot with my brothers, and my boastful pride and overconfidence rubbed salt into their wounds. I must learn to be more considerate of other people's feelings. But my brothers also need to be shown how it feels to be treated the way they've treated me.*

As Joseph trudged along beside the wagon, he thought through things he had done wrong and considered how he could have handled situations better. Though the seventeen-year-old boy still longed to get even with his brothers, he realized he'd have little opportunity to escape if he whined, complained, and came across as a spoiled brat. Joseph therefore used his month of walking to Egypt as a time to begin maturing and growing into a man God could better use for divine purposes.

Since Joseph would need to learn the language of a new land, he also tried to position himself around persons who could speak both Hebrew and Egyptian so that he began to pick up words and phrases of the new language he would need to learn.

Joseph had been stripped of all his worldly possessions. He would be entering Egypt with no tunic, no money, no friends or family, no references, no credentials, no reputation, and almost no knowledge of the Egyptian culture or language. Not only did he not have a penny to his name, but he didn't even have a name that was worth a penny — at least to the Egyptians.

Joseph thought about all he had suddenly lost. Did he still have anything besides an overbearing self-assurance that had been harshly treated by a strong dose of reality?

Yes. Yes, I do. I still have my character, I still have my faith, and I still have my destiny as a child of God. If my Lord will stay with me and direct my path, and if I allow him to work through me, I firmly believe that we can find a way to make something good out of this mess.

I resolve that it won't end this way. I'm not going to spend the rest of my life as a lowly slave. God has given me a vision of my destiny, and that vision was repeated and reaffirmed. I've been called to be more and do more—but I've got to do my part and take advantage of whatever opportunities God allows me to have. I need to work hard, trust God, and follow his leadership.

Joseph sighed, bowed his head, and prayed, "Help me, Lord. Lead me, guide me, teach me what you want me to learn in order to make me into the man you want me to be."

Chapter 3

Joseph stood at the back of a stage with other slaves waiting to be sold. Each of the slaves wore individual chains that extended from that prisoner's legcuff or shackle to a large chain anchored to the floor.

He had spent the preceding three days in a large cage that served as a holding area for slaves awaiting today's auction. During that time various potential buyers had poked, prodded, and examined him. Most of the examinations had been primarily physical in nature, since those buyers were looking for slaves that were healthy and strong enough to do the physical labor their jobs would require.

When Joseph's time came, he was unfastened from the large chain and led to an auction block, which was a raised platform at the front of the stage in full view of the audience of potential buyers. The auctioneer began jabbering loudly in a language Joseph was only beginning to learn—and the words seemed hopelessly jumbled together and were spoken far too quickly for him to understand.

Joseph therefore shifted his attention to the persons bidding on him. The early bids seemed to be primarily from a couple of men who had looked him over and jabbed Joseph while he was in the large cage. He remembered how they had examined his muscles and felt his backbone. *Probably farmers or agricultural workers.*

About the time one of the farmers dropped out of the bidding, another man got involved. Judging from his attire, Joseph guessed that he might be a caravan wagon master. *If he buys me, I might have a better chance of escaping.*

A man dressed like an Egyptian military officer moved up close to the auction block and made a bid. At the sight of him, the caravan master turned and melted into the crowd, the farmer ceased bidding, and Joseph was sold to the officer.

Joseph was led from the auction block to another holding area near the stage, where he was met by two men.

One was the Egyptian official who had bought him, while the other was one of the men who had closely examined Joseph while he was in the cage two days earlier. In addition to checking his physical characteristics, the man had also quizzed Joseph in Hebrew on a variety of subjects.

That man stepped forward, bowed slightly and said, "My name is Hadid. You have been purchased by Potiphar, Pharaoh's chief steward and captain of the guard." He nodded toward the Egyptian military officer. "You will work with me while I teach you the Egyptian language. Then our master will assign you to a more appropriate position."

"I understand," Joseph said.

Chapter 4

Joseph was taken to a massive structure that was apparently where Potiphar lived. Since Joseph had lived in tents and simple structures all his life, he at first assumed the structure must be an inn or similar building that housed numerous families—but Hadid assured him that this was not the case. It was the house where Potiphar and his wife lived with their servants and slaves.

Since Hadid's regular duties consisted primarily of working in the stables, Joseph worked alongside him while learning the Egyptian language. He fed and watered the horses, helped sweep and clean the stalls, and repaired or replaced boards as needed. As they worked together, Hadid instructed Joseph regarding the Egyptian names for different objects and ways to say various phrases. Whenever commands were given, Hadid would translate the command into Hebrew and then have Joseph repeat the words to him in the Egyptian language.

One day Joseph asked Hadid, "Don't you get tired of having to spend so much time teaching me both my basic duties and a new language?"

"Not at all," he replied. "Teaching Egyptian to new foreign slaves is one of my primary duties, since I am fluent in six languages. In fact, that's probably why Potiphar bought me. Besides, it's easier work than the physical labor I am otherwise required to do, and I enjoy it more—especially when I am blessed with a student who is as intelligent and as good a worker as you are."

"Thanks for the compliments. What type of man is our master?"

"He's a strict taskmaster and a brave warrior. But you'd expect that in the captain of Pharaoh's bodyguard—especially since he is also the country's chief executioner. He expects quick and complete compliance with his orders, but he is also fair, decent, and honest. You could have done much worse than to be chosen as his slave."

"I suspect you had something to do with my being chosen by him."

Hadid started to grin slightly before bending down to adjust his sandal. "Well, yes. Helping my master choose prospective slaves is one of my duties. Anyone can gauge their physical characteristics. My ability to speak foreigners' languages gives me an advantage in determining their intelligence, aptitude, and how well they will fit in with this household. Obey your commands and you'll do well here."

Chapter 5

When Joseph had sufficiently learned the Egyptian language to work apart from Hadid, he was moved into Potiphar's house, where he initially helped the kitchen slaves and cleaned the house. The servants and slaves worked and slept on the first floor of the house, while Potiphar's family occupied the upper floors.

Joseph learned his duties, diligently applied himself, worked hard, and pretended that everything he was asked or commanded to do was being done for the Lord.

He prayed when he lay down each night, thanking God for leading him through that day and asking for the Lord's guidance and direction. *You have shown me visions of what I am to become. I can't achieve any of it as a lowly slave or without your help. I must trust you to have your way in my life — but that requires me to put myself fully into your hands and to turn all aspects of my life over to you. Please help me learn what you would have me to know so that I might be ready and able to do the tasks you have for me.*

Over the next several months Joseph was given greater and greater responsibilities and more important duties. He got along well with the other slaves, he continued to learn the language and customs, and his labor resulted in ever-increasing success.

One day Shoshen, the slave who supervised Joseph's work, approached him and said, "Come with me." He led Joseph to the elaborate gardens that were adjacent to the house, pointed to the small building at the center of the gardens, and said, "Our master wants to visit with you in there."

After quizzing Joseph about his background, family, and personal information, Potiphar smiled wryly and said, "So you're here as a slave in a foreign land with no friends, no family, no money, and no apparent future. But you don't appear to be depressed or bitter about it. Why is that?"

"I firmly believe that my life and my future are in the hands of my God."

"Which god is that?"

"The God of my fathers—my ancestors. In my native Hebrew language, we call him Elohim. He has shown me that he has a plan and purpose for my life, but it's up to me to work, learn and prepare myself to be ready to move through the doors he will open for me at the right time. I may not understand how being a lowly slave fits into God's plan, but God knows—and that's good enough for me. My job is to obey your commands as if they were from God and trust him to do the rest."

Potiphar sat still and stared intently

at Joseph before leaning forward and saying, "As of this moment, you are no longer just a lowly slave. You're still my slave, but you'll also be my personal attendant. You'll report to me first thing each morning and will do whatever task you are assigned. Your duties will probably vary from day to day and week to week. Come with me and I'll show you where to report each morning."

Potiphar led Joseph back into the house, informed Shoshen of Joseph's new position, and led him up the stairs to the second floor. "You will now be allowed on this floor in order to carry out your duties. Report to me each morning in here," and he showed him a private room.

That night Joseph thanked God for

his new position. *Thank you, Lord, for remaining near me even during these difficult times, for giving me strength, and for being my guardian and guide. Please teach me what you'd have me learn.*

Chapter 6

Joseph's duties as Potiphar's personal attendant did indeed vary substantially from day to day and week to week. Some days he was little more than an errand boy, fetching items for his master or taking messages to someone. But there were other times when he was required to do things he didn't really think he had the knowledge, skills, or training to adequately perform the mission he had been assigned. On those occasions Joseph made certain he sought the Lord's wisdom and guidance, and he was careful to follow God's leadership and direction—even if he didn't understand why God was leading him in a particular way.

Joseph's successes in those endeavors emphasized to him that he could rely on the Lord for guidance. Potiphar also took notice of how his new Hebrew slave seemed to be able to accomplish tasks that should have been beyond his capabilities. As a result, Potiphar gradually increased Joseph's duties so that he became more than just a personal attendant. Any task he assigned to the young man would be carried out not just to the best of Joseph's abilities, but seemingly even beyond those abilities. Potiphar often caught himself shaking his head in wonder and muttering to himself, "That boy is phenomenal!"

When Raeus, the overseer of Potiphar's household, was caught embezzling funds, Potiphar only paused momentarily before ordering that Raeus be executed, and then he gave the now vacated position of overseer to Joseph.

Potiphar took Joseph throughout his estate, instructed him on his new duties, and introduced him to all his other slaves and servants. Many of them had worked with Joseph over the preceding months, of course, but now they would be under his command and direction. Potiphar wanted to make certain they knew Joseph would be in control of the household and would be giving them orders.

Joseph then took the time to visit with the individual slaves and servants, listening as they explained their duties to him, and watching as they demonstrated certain tasks. He asked if they had ideas of how they could accomplish their duties more efficiently and made his own mental notes. He gathered the written records kept by Raeus and others, took them to the private office and bedroom he would now occupy, and studied them. Then he spent time praying and seeking God's direction and guidance.

Chapter 7

Joseph promoted Hadid to be in charge of the stables, the horses, and the other livestock. Shoshen continued to oversee the household slaves and servants, and the agricultural master Neptah was placed in control of the fields and farms. Joseph delegated sufficient powers to each supervisor for them to be in charge of their respective operations, though each reported to Joseph and followed his instructions.

As the overall business manager, Joseph was responsible for all of

Potiphar's possessions. He purchased new equipment and supplies as needed, entered into contracts for the sale of crops and other products, and saw to the health and well being of the slaves and servants under his direction and control. If either Potiphar or his wife, Zuleikha, desired entertainment, Joseph arranged for musicians, jugglers, or other entertainers to perform for them. He oversaw parties and similar social gatherings for Potiphar.

Although Potiphar initially directed Joseph and gave him suggestions, he soon found this young Hebrew slave had competence and abilities far beyond his years and experience. *Perhaps his god actually does give him guidance and direction. I wish my gods would do the same for me. But maybe one or more of them did when I bought this kid. Or maybe it was the kid's god.*

Within a few weeks of Joseph's promotion to overseer, Potiphar's affairs were running smoother than they ever had before. In fact, he found that he no longer had to concern himself with any of his household duties other than the food he ate—and that may have been only because he had particular dietary practices that forbade a person of a different race or ethnicity from controlling what he ate. Nevertheless, he entrusted Joseph with every other aspect of his household management, and God continued to be with Joseph and to bless all that Potiphar owned.

Although still a slave, Joseph had the power to assign and reassign duties as he saw fit. Merchants reported to him, and he could sell crops and livestock for the prices he negotiated. Within months the household was making a profit with the income generated exceeding the expenses incurred. Under Joseph's direction, Potiphar was becoming even more wealthy than ever before. God's blessings were upon them, which made the master of the house happy.

Potiphar's wife also took notice of Joseph. At first it may have been largely a matter of convenience, since Joseph was in charge of the household. But she had already noticed the handsome Hebrew slave her husband had purchased, and she kept her eye on him when given the opportunity. After Joseph was promoted to being overseer of the household, Zuleikha finally had legitimate reasons for being in contact with him.

There were occasions when she could send for him or have him do something for her. There were also times when they could have a friendly talk. They each were intelligent and had outgoing personalities. Both were exceptionally good looking. As a high-ranking government official, Potiphar had his choice of beautiful women. He chose Zuleikha as his trophy wife, and she had chosen Joseph as the man who most attracted her, since he was well-built and good to look at. They would make a very good-looking couple—and Potiphar's wife knew it.

At first she tried mild flirtations: a beautiful smile, a come-hither glance, a seductive pose, lightly brushing up against him while passing each other in a hallway or while taking a tray from him—just little "innocent" things to help him notice the gorgeous woman in his presence. Minor flirtation was all it had ever taken for Zuleikha to turn a man's head in the past.

And Joseph turned his head. He noticed her. But instead of taking the hint and coming to her, he made extra efforts to keep his distance from her. He even appointed another slave to be her personal attendant and to tend to her individual needs.

But what Potiphar's wife felt she

needed most was Joseph himself—and that couldn't be provided by someone else.

Zuleikha considered her options. *Perhaps that Hebrew slave is a bit dense. I may have to be more direct with him than I'm accustomed to being with Egyptian men.* She took an ornate alabaster vase to Joseph and asked him to fill it with water and bring it to her bedroom on the top floor. Joseph handed the vase to the slave he had appointed to be Zuleikha's personal attendant and had that slave fill the vase and take it to Potiphar's wife.

One day she caught Joseph alone in a room on the second floor of the house. "Joseph, I need to talk with you for a moment," she said.

"All right."

"I need to know if something's wrong, Joseph."

"What do you mean?"

"We had quite a few delightful conversations back when you first became overseer of my household, but lately you've been avoiding me. Why?"

"I haven't been avoiding you . . . except for those times when no one else would be around."

"Why those times?"

"I want to make certain our relationship remains as it should be. I'm a slave and you are my master's wife."

"That means I am also your master and you should do what I tell you to do."

"What do you want?"

"I want *you,* Joseph. I want you to come lie down in my bed with me."

"I can't do that, Mrs. Potiphar."

"My name is Zuleikha. Call me by my name."

"I must not lie down with you, Zuleikha."

"Why? Am I not attractive enough for you?"

"You're the most beautiful woman I've ever known."

"Then take me, Joseph. I order you as your master to lie down and enjoy being together."

"That's the one thing I cannot do.

You are the wife of my master."

"He'll never know. He's out of town and won't be back for two days. It will be our secret. Don't you deserve a break from all your work? I'm yours for the taking."

"You're a lovely lady, but you're also married to my master. He's the man who must meet your needs." Joseph got up and hurried from the room.

He sat down in a thicket of trees adjoining one of Potiphar's fields and thought through Zuleikha's offer. It was definitely tempting. He *had* been working hard and could certainly use a break. He'd been through a lot: betrayed by his own brothers, sold into slavery, destitute, maligned, neglected. He was lonely and longed for a woman's kisses, embraces — and more. His master's wife was the most gorgeous woman he'd ever seen — and she wanted him. He could even justify it because he was also her slave and would merely be following her orders.

She claimed that no one would ever know. It would be their own private secret. But they would both know that they had cheated. And God would know.

Yeah, Joseph wanted it. He was a normal man with hormones that longed for him to be sexually joined to a woman. God made men to be sexually stimulated by pretty women, and Potiphar had chosen a very beautiful woman to be his wife. But she was *his* wife — not Joseph's.

And Joseph knew that God's will was for him to save himself for when he would unite himself with his own wife... whenever that might be. *God, please give me the wisdom to know your will, the strength to do it, and the perseverance to stay the course in the way you would have me to go.*

Chapter 8

Zuleikha continued her flirtations and attempts to seduce Joseph. When other people were around, her attempts were rather subtle: a seductive smile, a wink of an eye, a slight nod of the head or change of facial expression. If no one else was near, she might brush against him or ask if he had reconsidered her offer. Joseph always remained friendly and well-mannered, but he also continually refused her advances and invitations.

One day she confronted Joseph more directly. "I can't understand why you repeatedly reject me, Joseph. Why don't you do what I tell you to do? Am I that distasteful to you?"

"Don't you understand?" Joseph replied. "My master — your husband — has placed his entire estate in my hands to manage and maintain. He trusts me to do what is right and good for him. He gives no thought to anything in this house, and all that he owns he has placed in my hands. He has withheld nothing from me except you, since you are his wife. How then could I betray his trust and do this most wicked thing? Having sexual relations with you would violate his trust in both of us and would also be a sin before God."

Although Joseph's words seemed to get through to Zuleikha so that Joseph was able to walk out of the room while she considered what he had said, within a couple of days she was back to coaxing him to meet her in her bedroom.

One day Potiphar's wife found Joseph working on the second floor of the house while no other servant or slave was around. She caught him by his outer garment and said, "Lie with me!" Joseph attempted to break free from her grasp, but she held on too tightly for him to do so. He therefore twisted around, slipping out of the garment and leaving it with her.

This was a new experience for Zuleikha. She was accustomed to having men almost fall over each other trying to win her favor. *How dare that Hebrew slave turn me down! Does he really think he's better than me? I could have his head for this, and my husband can deliver it for me. That'll teach that uppity slave who is really boss around here.*

When Zuleikha saw that Joseph had left his clothing with her and had fled outside, she screamed loudly, staggered from the room she was in, and was met by five household servants who responded to her screams. She waved Joseph's cloak and said, "Look, my husband had to bring us a Hebrew to mock and play with us! This one attacked me and tried to lie with me, but when I screamed, he ran away and fled outside."

She kept Joseph's clothing beside her until Potiphar came home. Then she showed it to him as she repeated her story. Zuleikha held up the garment and said, "That Hebrew slave you brought into our house tried to rape me today — but when I screamed at the top of my voice and grabbed his clothing, he left this with me and fled outside."

Potiphar took Joseph's cloak, examined it, and threw it to the ground. Eyes blazing, he turned and stalked from the room, went to the garden adjacent to his house, and paced back and forth there while he collected his thoughts. Then he went to a couple of the soldiers who guarded the entry to his house and commanded them to arrest Joseph and take him to the prison under his direct control.

Chapter 9

"You wished to see me, sir?" asked the chief jailer of the prison where the Pharaoh's prisoners were kept.

"Yes, Rajib," answered Potiphar. "We've known each other for many years and have worked together closely for the last several. I have a personal favor to ask of you, but I want it to be kept quiet. Don't tell anyone else."

"What is it?"

"My soldiers are delivering a new prisoner to your prison."

"Who is it?"

"His name is Joseph. He's the Hebrew slave I had made overseer of my household."

"Another one? Didn't you have your last overseer executed?"

"Yes. That one was caught embezzling funds."

"What did this one do?"

"My wife says he tried to rape her."

"When's his execution?"

"There's none scheduled—and there might not be one."

"I don't understand. You execute your overseer for embezzling—but not for trying to rape your wife?"

"I don't know whether to believe Zuleikha. I've never had a slave whose integrity impressed me more than Joseph. But I've also never met a woman more beautiful or seductive than the girl I married. So I don't know, Rajib, and I'm not sure I want to know."

"What's the slave's side of the story?"

"I haven't talked to him. I'm afraid of what he might say."

Rajib raised his eyebrows. Then he nodded and said, "Yeah. No matter which one is actually the victim, you had to separate them. And you still need to live with your wife."

"True—but separating them has cost me the best overseer I've ever had."

"Ah, so that's the real reason you want me to watch him."

"You always were perceptive, Rajib. You've been needing someone to help you here in the prison. I'll leave it to you as to whether my slave might be of assistance."

Chapter 10

When the jail door slammed shut, it made a dull metallic thud that reverberated both in the jail corridors and in the corridors of Joseph's mind, heralding the end of his grandiose dreams. Gone were the necklace and ring of Potiphar's overseer. A heavy bronze collar had replaced the necklace, and metal fetters bound his ankles.

Joseph looked around and shook his head. The cell was a tiny, dingy room whose floor and walls were caked with filth. The smell of human excrement burned his nostrils and made his eyes water. *Is this my reward for trying to do my best for my master? He throws me into this tiny cell, locks me up, and throws away the key!*

No, he still has the key — and he just might use it to take me out and string me up. After all, he is Egypt's chief executioner. Remember what he did to his prior overseer. But Raeus was caught embezzling funds, while I did nothing wrong.

Yeah, but my master's wife accused me of trying to rape her. BUT I DIDN'T. I resisted her seductions and rebuffed her advances. I was faithful and true to my master and didn't violate his trust — and he still throws me into prison. That's so unfair!

No, that's life. It wasn't fair for my brothers to sell me into slavery. But it also wasn't fair for Dad to pamper me and favor me over my brothers. Life isn't always fair. So deal with it — and learn from it.

Joseph sank to his knees and leaned against one of the walls in the tiny cell. He took a deep breath, exhaled and breathed a brief prayer. *God, please be with me and help me learn the lessons you would have me know so that I can become the man you want me to be.*

Rajib took the bronze collar and fetters off Joseph, moved him to a better room where he could watch him, and was favorably impressed by what he saw. Perhaps more importantly, the Lord watched over Joseph and was with him. It wasn't long before Rajib began giving

Joseph minor duties around the prison, and the young man performed all tasks well.

Soon the chief jailer put Joseph in charge of all the prisoners in the prison so that he was responsible for everything that was done there.

Joseph had previously shown his aptitude and talent for working with slaves and servants who were in Potiphar's household. But those were persons who were generally willing to work and take orders. Now he was faced with the task of working with sullen, disrespectful, and rebellious men who had generally committed one or more crimes. Those who had been condemned to die had nothing to lose by the way they behaved or misbehaved.

Instead of sinking into a deep depression and having his own private pity party, Joseph again decided to act as if his prison assignments were from God and that they were being used to help him develop his organizational and managerial skills as well as his ability to work with people. Once again, God saw to it that those skills were recognized and rewarded, giving Joseph success in all that he did.

After Joseph had been in charge of the other prisoners for several months, Pharaoh's chief baker and cupbearer were thrown into the prison that was under Potiphar and Rajib's control, and Joseph was assigned to take care of them. Both men remained in the prison while an investigation was conducted as to who was responsible for poisoning some of Pharaoh's food. Both men had ample opportunity to have done it, of course, since one of them cooked the food and the other one served it to the king.

After they had been in custody for some time, Joseph discovered one morning that both men were downcast and depressed. "What's wrong?" he asked.

"We both had similar dreams last night which have troubled us greatly, since we don't know what they mean," the cupbearer said.

"Yes," said the baker. "Two dreams with similarities occurring the same night are omens that something important is about to happen, but we can't figure out the meaning—and there is no one here who can interpret them."

Joseph responded, "Surely God can interpret your dreams. If you tell me your dreams, perhaps God will reveal the meaning to me."

The cupbearer said, "In my dream, there was a vine in front of me. On the vine were three branches. It had barely budded when out came its blossoms and its clusters ripened into grapes. Since Pharaoh's cup was in my hand, I took the grapes, pressed them into Pharaoh's cup, and placed the cup into Pharaoh's hand."

Joseph mentally prayed, *Lord, please illuminate me, guide me, and give me your wisdom and insight*—and the branches of grapes became days of the week, while the cupbearer's actions became tasks he would perform when released from his prison cell.

Joseph said to him, "This is its interpretation: The three branches represent three days. In three days, Pharaoh will pardon you and restore you to your post. You will place Pharaoh's cup into his hand, as was your custom formerly when you were his cupbearer.

"But think of me when all is well with you again and do me the kindness of mentioning me to Pharaoh, so as to free me from this place. I was kidnapped from the land of the Hebrews and have done nothing here that is either illegal or immoral so that I should have been confined to prison."

"Oh, I certainly will," said the cupbearer. "If your interpretation is true and I am returned to my former position as Pharaoh's personal servant, I'll be more than happy to tell him about you and see if he won't get you out of here."

When the chief baker saw how favorably his cellmate's dream had been interpreted, he said to Joseph, "In my dream, similarly, there were three openwork baskets on my head. In the uppermost basket were all kinds of food for Pharaoh that a baker prepares, and birds were eating it out of the basket above my head."

Joseph answered, "This is its interpretation. The three baskets are also three days. In three days, Pharaoh will lift off your head and impale you upon a pole—and the birds will pick off your flesh."

The baker's eyes filled with terror at Joseph's words. He glanced at his cell mate but found no comfort there.

Three days later marked Pharaoh's birthday. He ordered that a banquet be prepared for all his officials. Both the cupbearer and baker were released from prison. The cupbearer was restored to his prior position so that he was able to place the king's cup into Pharaoh's hand—but the baker was impaled on a pole just as Joseph had said.

When Joseph heard the news, he offered a quick prayer thanking God for making it possible for him to correctly interpret the dreams of both men. He wondered how quickly Pharaoh would be told about him and what the king's response would be. Would Pharaoh listen? Would he have compassion? Would he even care? Joseph at least had a hope for the future, and he began making some contingent plans while waiting for the time he would be released from prison—and he wondered if that would end his status as slave.

Would he be free again? If so, would he remain in Egypt, return to Canaan, or go somewhere else? Unless God revealed the answers ahead of time, Joseph would just have to wait. So he waited.

And waited.

And waited some more. Days turned into weeks, weeks into months, and the months dragged by while he waited.

But the young man wasn't idle. He used the time to work on his organization and management skills while assisting the prison's chief jailer. Once again God blessed his labor and made his efforts successful.

It's not always easy being in God's waiting room, but that's where Joseph was—and he found that the time seemed to go by more quickly and with more satisfactory results when he spent the time productively rather than just sitting back wishing Pharaoh would get him out of prison even though Joseph had no control over that occurring.

Chapter 11

Joseph didn't note anything particularly special about The Day when he woke up that morning. Not at first, anyway. Not until he heard a stirring at the entrance to the prison--followed by Rajib running up to Joseph, grabbing him, and telling him to hurry.

"What's happening?" asked Joseph.

"The king's guards are here to take you to Pharaoh."

"Why?"

"I don't know, but they're in a hurry—so it must be important."

"What does it usually mean when Pharaoh sends for a prisoner?"

Rajib caught his breath, looked away while shaking his head, and muttered, "I don't want to say."

"That bad?"

Rajib nodded, still looking away.

"Execution?"

Another nod.

"They asked for me?"

"Well, they wanted to know if a Hebrew was still here. You're the only Hebrew who has been here in years—so it must be you."

"Give me a moment," Joseph said. When Rajib nodded approval, Joseph bowed his head and prayed, "Lord, please be with me. Guide my words and my actions so that they conform to your will for my life."

Joseph went with the men, who took him to a room in the palace where he was stripped, bathed, shaved, and given a haircut and new clothing. Gone were his soiled prison rags, replaced by a new white robe and sandals.

When the attendants had finished with Joseph, the guards reappeared and escorted him to Pharaoh's throne room. Joseph had previously been awed by the magnificence of Potiphar's residence, but that paled in comparison with the grandeur of Pharaoh's throne room. The ceiling arched high overhead, sunlight flooded into the room through huge open-air windows near the ceiling, and brightly colored hieroglyphs adorned the walls. Magnificent gold and stone statues and columns towered above him and a rich plush carpet stretched from where Joseph stood at the entrance to the room to the base of a dais from which rose the impressive throne upon which Pharaoh sat.

The king stretched out his scepter toward Joseph, and the guards on either side of him marched him forward. They stopped when they got to the dais, and Joseph got a good look at the Egyptian monarch.

Pharaoh's bare chest was surrounded by rich garments interwoven with gold, silver and precious jewels. A rearing cobra was centered in a leather cone atop the king's head. He wore heavy eye makeup and a false beard. He glanced at his chief cupbearer, whom Joseph recognized as being the man he had met in prison two years earlier. ***Two years!*** At least he had finally remembered his promise to Joseph.

When the cupbearer nodded acknowledgement that this was the correct Hebrew man, Pharaoh leaned forward and said, "I have had dreams that concern me, but no one has been able to interpret them for me. Now I have heard it said that you merely have to hear a dream in order to correctly interpret its meaning."

Joseph replied, "Not I. It is God who

has sent Pharaoh his dream, and it is God who may provide its meaning. I am merely the mouthpiece God may choose to use."

Pharaoh smiled wryly and nodded. "Then let us hope your god chooses to use you. In my dream, I was standing by the bank of the Nile when out of the river came seven sturdy and well-formed cows that began grazing in the reed grass. Presently seven other cows followed them out of the Nile, but these cows were scrawny, ill-formed, and emaciated. Never had I seen their likes for ugliness in all the land of Egypt! And the seven lean and ugly cows ate up the first seven sturdy cows. But the seven ill-formed ugly cows remained just as emaciated as they had been before eating the good cows. That's when I woke up.

"When I finally went back to sleep, I had another dream that was just as troubling as the first one. In this dream I saw seven ears of grain, full and healthy, growing on a single stalk. Right behind them sprouted another stalk that had seven ears that were shriveled, thin, and scorched by the east wind. Then the thin ears of corn swallowed the seven healthy ears.

"I told my dreams to my soothsayers, priests, magicians, and wise men, but none of them were able to offer an interpretation for me."

Joseph said to the king, "Pharaoh's dreams are actually one and the same. God has told Pharaoh what he is about to do. The seven healthy cows are seven years, and the seven healthy ears of grain are seven years; it is the same dream told twice using different symbolism. Similarly, the seven lean and ugly cows that followed are also seven years, as are the seven empty ears of grain scorched by the east wind; they are seven years of famine.

"It is just as I have told Pharaoh: God has revealed to you what he is about to do. Immediately ahead are seven years of great abundance in all the land of Egypt. After them will come seven years of famine so severe that all the abundance during the good years will be forgotten. As Egypt is ravaged by famine, no trace of the abundance will be left in the land because the famine will be so severe. As for Pharaoh having had the same dream twice, it means the matter has been determined by God and that he will soon carry it out."

Pharaoh, his advisors, and all others who heard Joseph's words sat or stood in stunned silence. "Famine" was worse than just a dirty word. Any famine would be a disaster for a country whose economy was based upon agriculture. A seven-year famine could bring Egypt to its knees. It was simply an unthinkable prospect.

Joseph broke the silence by offering a solution. "Accordingly, let Pharaoh find a man of discernment and wisdom, and set him over the land of Egypt. Let Pharaoh take steps to appoint overseers and officers over the land and organize the agricultural production during the seven years of plenty. Let these officers take one-fifth of the harvest during each of the seven good years, pile up the grain in storage facilities, and keep it as a reserve in the various cities of Egypt so that the kingdom might not be ruined by the famine."

The plan pleased Pharaoh, his advisors and courtiers. Pharaoh turned to them and said, "Could we find another man like this one—a man in whom is the spirit of God?"

Pharaoh then turned back to Joseph and said, "Since God has made all this known to you, it appears to me that there is no other person as discerning and wise as you. I therefore decree that you shall oversee my court and my people. By your command shall all my people be directed. Only with respect to the throne shall I be superior to you."

Pharaoh beckoned Joseph to ascend the dais and stand directly before him. Removing his signet ring from his hand, Pharaoh put it on one of Joseph's fingers and said, "See, I am putting you in charge of all the land of Egypt."

Pharaoh turned to his attendants, snapped his fingers and said, "Dress Joseph in the finest linen robes and put a royal gold chain about his neck. Give him my number two chariot, since he is now my second-in-command, and make ready a royal residence for him."

Pharaoh had effectively reversed the

playing field: Now it was Joseph who stood before the king in stunned silence. As long as he had been speaking words that God directed him to say, he spoke with amazing confidence that bordered on chutzpah. But Pharaoh's response of moving Joseph from a prison cell to being the second most powerful man in all of Egypt was such a meteoric rise that the young man was left dumbstruck.

"In order to carry out your new duties, you will need Egyptian citizenship and an Egyptian name," Pharaoh continued. He turned to his court scribe and said, "Prepare the necessary documents giving him full citizenship rights and authority. Also note that on official state documents Joseph may bear the name of

Zaphennath-paneah, which signifies that he is the man to whom mysteries are revealed and will be the nourisher of life in Egypt."

Pharaoh clapped his hands twice and ordered, "See to it. Now!"

Attendants immediately took Joseph by his arms and led him from the throne room. Tailors measured him for his new linen garments.

As they finished with Joseph, the chief tailor motioned to a young man who came forward, bowed to Joseph, and said, "My name is Deshoris. Pharaoh has appointed me to be your charioteer. Please come with me."

Deshoris led Joseph to a royal chariot pulled by two beautiful white horses.

Again bowing, Deshoris motioned for Joseph to get aboard the chariot.

"Wow!" Joseph exclaimed. "Is this for me?"

"Yes, Sire. I am to take you to your new home."

As they rode through the streets of the city, people bowed reverently as they passed, which was a new experience for Joseph. They stopped in front of a magnificent edifice.

"Welcome to your new home, Sire," said Deshoris.

A shocked Joseph stood mutely gazing at the building in front of him. Although similar in size to the residence of Potiphar, it was more regal and elegant than his old master's house.

Realizing his mouth was hanging open, Joseph exhaled while composing himself and muttered, "All this is for me?"

"Yes, Sire. After all, you are now the second most powerful ruler in all the land of Egypt."

Joseph took a deep breath and shook his head before slowly exhaling and climbing down from his chariot. He wandered wide-eyed through the house, hardly daring to believe it would be his new home. His examination of the second floor was interrupted by Deshoris' excited voice calling to him from the entrance, "Sire, where are you?"

"Here I am. What do you need?"

Deshoris motioned toward a military

war chariot bearing two men and said, "Pharaoh has summoned you to go with these officers to the palace immediately."

When Joseph arrived at the palace, he was rushed to a room where attendants dressed him in a royal robe, placed a heavy gold chain around his neck, and put a gem-studded headdress on his head.

Guards then led him back to the throne room. When Pharaoh stretched out his scepter, Joseph and his accompanying guards approached the throne.

Pharaoh motioned for Joseph to come closer, and the young man climbed the dais and bowed before his king.

"Have you had a chance to see your

new house and chariot?"

"Yes, Sire. Thank you."

"Now it's time for you to meet your new wife."

"Wife?"

"Yes. Your new wife. I have decreed that you will marry Asenath, the daughter of Poti-phera, the priest of On."

"When?"

"Now."

"Now?"

"Yes. Immediately. I've summoned them and they arrived shortly before you got here."

"Isn't this rather sudden? I mean, I've never even seen her or—"

"Joseph, listen carefully," the king

whispered while leaning closer to the young man. "If your interpretation of my dream is correct—and I have no reason to doubt that it is—you will need to begin taking immediate actions to keep the coming disaster from destroying Egypt. We don't have time for others to question your authority.

"Naming you as my second in command gives you political authority, but you also need proper high-ranking social standing. As Ra's high priest, Potiphera has social standing that is almost equal to mine. Marrying his daughter will give you instant social prestige. She's also beautiful, intelligent and charming. You could definitely do worse."

Pharaoh paused before giving Joseph

a hard look and adding, "Besides—since I decreed that the two of you will marry each other immediately, neither of you really has a choice in the matter. So make the best of it."

"Yes, Sire."

Pharaoh sat up straight on his throne, turned slightly toward his left, and stretched out his scepter in that direction. Joseph turned and watched as a man and a woman walked slowly toward the throne. The man wore elaborate priestly garments with a breastplate encrusted with jewels, while the woman was attired in a white linen dress and a purple amethyst necklace with golden highlights. A matching bracelet adorned her left wrist. Both wore worried expressions on their faces as they moved to a point directly in front of the king's throne and prostrated themselves.

"Rise," Pharaoh commanded.

Both the man and the woman stood up and faced their king.

"You understand my decree, don't you?" Pharaoh asked.

They both nodded.

Pharaoh addressed the priest, "Then proceed."

Poti-phera sighed and stepped up onto the royal dais as Joseph stepped down off of it.

Joseph cast a furtive glance at the woman standing next to him. *She looks as nervous as I feel. Oh God, help us. Lead us, guide us, and bless us. And please don't hold it against me that I am marrying a pagan woman who doesn't know or worship you. If possible, please become her God as well.*

Joseph opened his eyes, realizing that he had tuned everything out while mentally praying—and apparently the priest had already started the marriage ceremony. Worse, he must have asked Joseph a question and was now waiting for an answer.

"Uh—er—a—what?"

"Do you accept this woman as your wife and agree to be responsible for her?'

"Uh—yes—I do."

Poti-phera turned toward his daughter and asked, "And do you agree to be this man's wife and to submit yourself to him?"

"Yes." Asenath turned to Joseph and said, "I pledge myself to you, and am now yours."

"Then by my authority under the laws of Egypt and as priest of Ra, I ask Ra's blessings upon your union, and I proclaim you to be husband and wife according to the laws of Egypt."

Joseph turned toward his new wife and said, "This seems both awkward and backwards since we are now officially married—but perhaps it would be a good idea if we introduced ourselves to each other." He paused while flashing a wry grin at Asenath. "My name is Joseph."

"So I've heard. It's nice to meet you." The corners of her mouth curled upwards in the briefest of smiles that at least succeeded in softening her worried look as she added, "Or at least I hope it is, since we are now bound to one another. My name is Asenath—and this is my father."

Joseph looked at Poti-phera, but the priest had a guarded expression on his face that Joseph was unable to read.

Pharaoh pointed his scepter at his court scribe and beckoned him to come to the throne dais. He then asked Asenath, "Will you need help moving your belongings to your new home?"

"Probably, my Lord."

Turning to the scribe, Pharaoh said, "See to it that Asenath has whatever help she needs to move her belongings to Joseph's house today. After you assign the necessary men to get that done, visit with Joseph to find out what he needs to get started on his projects for saving Egypt from the coming famine."

Pharaoh smiled at Joseph. "If you need anything, Sarnack will be your contact person," and he motioned toward the scribe, who bowed his head slightly in Joseph's direction. Sarnack then led the others out of the throne room.

Chapter 12

Joseph leaned forward, looked into Asenath's eyes, and said softly, "Tell me about yourself."

The newlyweds sat in chairs facing each other in the anteroom to their bedroom suite on the third floor of Joseph's new home.

"What do you want to know?" Asenath asked while nervously fidgeting with her amethyst bracelet.

"I want to know anything you feel comfortable telling me. Perhaps more than you're actually comfortable telling."

When Asenath hesitated, Joseph leaned forward and took her hands in his. Smiling, he softly said, "In order for our marriage to be all that it can and should be, we are going to have to develop both love for each other and trust in each other. That can't be done without honest communication. I realize that neither of us will feel comfortable telling anything and everything to strangers—and let's face it: that's what we are at this time. But we can help each other get better acquainted. So tell me whatever you feel comfortable saying, but keep it honest and loving, if possible."

Asenath bit her lip, wrinkled her brow and nodded slowly before taking a deep breath and smiling. "I'll try. I'm twenty-three years old and am the youngest daughter of Poti-phera, the high priest of the Egyptian sun god Ra. He's the man who conducted our wedding ceremony.

"I have two sisters and a brother, all older than me and married. All of us enjoy music and can play various musical instruments. I primarily have played flutes, though I also like harps.

"My favorite hobby is art, though it's not always easy to get the supplies. Papyrus is often seasonal, while paints and charcoal are often in short supply.

"That's about all I can think of at the moment. What about you?"

Joseph took a deep breath, exhaled, and said, "I'm thirty years old and I grew up in a family with eleven brothers and one sister. When I was seventeen years old, I was—uh—captured by a gang of men and sold to a caravan of Ishmaelites, who brought me to Egypt and sold me as a slave.

"I was purchased by Potiphar, Pharaoh's chief executioner. I worked for him for a number of years.

"Two years ago I met Pharaoh's cupbearer, who seemed distressed because he had had a dream that seemed especially vivid to him but which he didn't understand. He told me the dream, and I interpreted its meaning for him.

"When Pharaoh had two dreams one night that neither he nor his wise men and advisors could interpret, his cupbearer told him about me, and—well,

I guess you know the rest."

Asenath cocked her head to one side and eyed Joseph closely before asking, "So why are you able to interpret dreams when even the king's magicians, soothsayers, priests and wise men were unable to do so? I mean . . . those are men who make a living doing that sort of thing. Yet they were baffled by Pharaoh's dreams. Are you really smarter than all of them?"

"I'm not, but I know One who is. And he told me the meaning of the dreams."

"I thought you were the one who interpreted the meanings."

"I am. But you need to understand that Pharaoh's dreams were different from the normal kind we generally have."

"What do you mean?"

"Our dreams are usually so vague and fuzzy that we quickly forget them. But both the cupbearer's dream and those that Pharaoh had were vivid and deeply etched into their consciousness and memory."

"Is that important?"

"Yes. It means those dreams were sent to them by God."

"Which god?"

"The one true God: Elohim, though he can also be called El Shaddai. He's the one I worship. God created this world and everything in it. He also made the sun, moon, and stars. Since he sent those dreams to Pharaoh, he knew their meaning. I was merely the mouthpiece

God used to interpret them."

Asenath cocked her head and eyed Joseph. Then she smiled and said, "Well, Pharaoh apparently considers you to be more than merely a mouthpiece."

"What do you mean?"

"He immediately promoted you to be the second highest ranking official in all of Egypt and gave you this house." She shrugged before adding, "And he gave me to you as well. Said my father and I had no choice in the matter."

"Yeah," Joseph agreed. "He told me I didn't have a choice, either—and that I should just make the best of it."

Asenath momentarily looked shocked but then started laughing. "You too?"

Joseph also laughed. "Yeah, me too. Both of our lives have suddenly been changed in ways neither of us saw coming. But in addition to marrying a beautiful girl I'd never seen before, I also now have a new job with new powers and responsibilities, a new citizenship, a new home, and even a new name."

"New name?"

"Yeah, and I don't even remember what it is."

Chapter 13

Joseph looked up as Deshoris bowed to him at the entryway to his study. He motioned to his charioteer to rise and said, "What do you need?"

"Sire, a man is here with the maps and other documents you asked Sarnack to get for you."

"Send him in."

Deshoris got to his feet, walked to the doorway, and motioned to someone in the hallway to come forward. A man who appeared to be a few years younger than Joseph entered the room carrying several scrolls.

Joseph pointed to a table and said, "Put them there. What do you have?"

"This is the map of Egypt you requested, and these are maps of the areas where almost all the grain is grown. This next scroll contains charts, graphs and figures showing how much grain has been produced in each area over the past several years, while this last scroll is a census of Egypt's cities and towns."

"Thank you," Joseph said. When the young man continued standing by the table, Joseph asked, "Is there anything else?"

"Sarnack said that if it meets with your approval, I am to remain as your aide so that you can conveniently send me back to him for anything else you may need."

"What's your name?"

"Rynar, Sire."

"Well, Rynar, let me ask you a question first. If I ask you to tell Sarnack or Pharaoh or someone else something that's not true or correct, would you do that for me?"

"If I am your slave, I don't know that I would have any choice in the matter. But I don't think you would really want me to do that—or if it would even be wise."

"Why not?"

"Because a man who would willingly lie *for* you would also be more likely to lie *to* you."

Joseph smiled. "Good answer. I think we will get along well together. Have a seat while I study these documents you brought me."

Joseph spent the next hour making notations on the maps and outlining where he needed to go and what he needed to see to determine how Egypt's agricultural production during the next seven years could sustain the country during the seven years of famine that would follow.

He then bowed his head and prayed, "Lord, you've shown me what's going to happen. Now please show me what I must do to implement your will for me and for Egypt. Guide my actions and help me be a proper instrument of your will.

"Thank you for removing me from prison and giving me this position. Now help me do your will while carrying out my responsibilities. Show me which people I can rely on and trust, and which ones will question my commands and attempt to disrupt my efforts.

"Everywhere I look I see obstacles. Please show me how to face them, and in what order. And again, thank you, Lord, for this new life with its new opportunities."

As Joseph read back over his notes, one thing became increasingly clear to him. *I told Pharaoh that grain should be stored during the good years in preparation for the bad ones—but I have never built a grainery and don't know anyone who has done it.*

Joseph turned to Rynar and said, "I need you to find out who are the best grainery builders in Egypt. Talk to Sarnack and anyone else you need to— but bring me the names and locations of who are the best people available to build grain storage facilities."

Joseph then told Deshoris to get the chariot ready while he grabbed his cloak, a map, and his notes.

Chapter 14

Joseph spent the first weeks in his new position getting to know his new wife, familiarizing himself with the map of Egypt and its major cities and agricultural areas, and bathing the entire project in prayer. He then personally inspected the fields and visited with the officials in charge of both agricultural production and population centers. He examined records and talked with common laborers as well as their bosses and overseers. He sought God's guidance and wisdom in all that he did, and soon had a rather comprehensive composite of which areas were being well run and which had been mismanaged.

Guided by both God and by his own investigations, Joseph reassigned persons to positions that maximized their skills and abilities. He created new positions as needed and eliminated or consolidated others.

Joseph also met with contractors who were experienced with building storage facilities for grain and other crops, he found suitable sites for building those facilities in the various Egyptian cities, and he oversaw their construction.

He imposed a special tax that allowed the Egyptian government to collect and store twenty percent of all grain grown and harvested. It was this tax that caused the first major challenge to Joseph's policies and leadership. Rynar told Joseph that Sarnack wanted to speak to him privately, informing him of the time and place.

When Joseph arrived, Sarnack said, "I thought you should know that several of the agricultural field masters who oversee major farms complained to Pharaoh about the new tax you have imposed."

"What did they say?"

"They pointed out that the harvests were already taxed and claimed the farms did not produce enough grain to allow an additional confiscation of one-fifth of the crops."

"What did Pharaoh say?"

"He told them that you had assured him that Egypt's farms would produce enough grain to allow twenty percent to be confiscated and stored."

"What was their response?"

"They laughed, mocked you, and said it would be insane to believe the rantings and predictions of a non-farmer about what their fields would produce."

"And Pharaoh said?"

"He said the twenty percent surtax is now the law and they had better comply. But then he added that he would evaluate the situation after the first year's harvests."

"Anything else?"

"Yes. I saw them making plans after they left the throne room. I don't know what the plans are, but I thought you should know about it so you could be better prepared."

"Thanks for the warning, Sarnack. Which fields and agricultural masters are involved?"

"If you will send Rynar to my office with the maps and scrolls I sent you, I will mark them with that information."

"Thank you. I'll do that."

Chapter 15

Rynar knocked on Joseph's door and asked, "You sent for me, Sire?"

"Yes, Rynar. I have a special assignment for you, but I want to go over it with you first. Several weeks ago Sarnack warned me that certain agricultural masters may attempt to avoid surrendering the grain Egypt will need to survive the coming drought. I have arranged for you to work in some fields where you can watch them. Report any illegal or suspicious activities to me."

"Why don't you just replace them with masters you trust?"

"Because they seem to be competent agricultural masters who know how to get good yields of grain from their land. I've kept close watch on their fields and know they're doing a good job—thus far. I won't penalize them if all they've done is to complain to Pharaoh about me or the tax I've imposed. But we can't allow them to avoid surrendering the excess grain. We've got to safely store that if Egypt is to survive the coming seven years of famine."

Chapter 16

While Joseph was overseeing the collection and storage of grain, he saw Sarnack's chariot approaching.

"I bring you greetings from Pharaoh," the court scribe said as his chariot pulled next to Joseph's.

"And how is my Lord?" Joseph asked.

"He is doing well. He asked me to check with you regarding the first year's harvests."

"They are going well. Although we have not quite completed harvesting all the grain, this is already the best year on record. It appears that most of the fields have produced almost a third more grain than their average yield."

"In other words, even after you take twenty percent, the farmers still have more than normal."

"That is correct."

"What about the ones I told you might be plotting against you?"

"Ah, that's where it gets interesting," Joseph said. "For some reason their fields only seem to be up about ten percent over their prior average production."

"And why is that?"

"I have my suspicions, but I'd rather not say anything until I also have proof."

"Understood. Well, carry on."

Chapter 17

"Mighty Pharaoh," Joseph said as he bowed before the throne. "I have requested this audience in order to clear up a possible dispute or disagreement."

"Proceed," ordered the king as he tilted his scepter toward Joseph.

Pointing toward a group of men, Joseph said, "These men are some of Egypt's agricultural masters. It has come to my attention that they have formally objected to the twenty percent surtax I have levied on their fields. They claim that since you already tax them, we should not also confiscate one-fifth of their crops, which I have done to protect Egypt from the coming famine."

Turning toward the men, Joseph asked, "Have I correctly stated your position?"

"Yes," said one of the men while the others nodded. "Mighty Pharaoh, it is foolish to allow an alien who knows nothing about agriculture to make arbitrary rules your farmers must obey. Although our fields showed a slight increase this year, it was not enough to offset the surtax this madman imposed on us."

Joseph stepped forward carrying a scroll, which he showed to the men. "This is an accounting of what your fields produced, and these are your signatures attesting to the amounts and to the tax imposed upon them."

"Yes, that's correct."

"So it is your testimony that is the total amount your fields produced?"

"Yes — which is why we need relief from this excessive tax."

"Thank you," Joseph said while turning toward Sarnack. "Have the guards bring in the next witness."

A little man was escorted into the throne room by two big burly guards who stood on either side of him while his eyes nervously darted around the room. Joseph placed his hand on the man's left shoulder and said, "Tell Pharaoh your name."

"Rathebes."

"What is your profession?"

"I own a grain storage facility."

Joseph handed him a papyrus scroll and asked, "Are you familiar with this document?"

"Yes."

"What is it?"

"It's a receipt for wheat."

"Who owns the wheat?"

"Those men over there," and Rathebes pointed to the other men.

"Why did they store the wheat with you?"

"They wanted to hide it from the government—from you."

"Thank you. I have one more witness I

would like to present," Joseph said.

"Proceed," ordered Pharaoh.

"Have the guards bring in our last witness."

When that man joined Joseph before the throne, Joseph said, "Mighty Pharaoh, you may remember this man as being one of the agricultural masters who initially objected to the surtax I imposed. He differs from the others in that he refused to sign the accounting saying that was the full amount of crops produced by his fields."

Joseph turned to the man and asked, "Why did you refuse to sign?"

"I refused to sign because it would not have been honest or correct. I knew some of our crops had been hidden with

Rathebes."

Joseph turned back toward Pharaoh and said, "Because he confessed his actions and has repented, I ask that his only punishment be the forfeiture of his portion of the crops hidden with Rathebes."

Pharaoh smiled at Joseph, nodded and said, "Granted."

Chapter 18

"How are you feeling?" Joseph asked Asenath as he walked into the room where she was sitting.

"I'm doing well. I've just been nursing our newest son. Have you decided on a name yet?"

"Yes. I'd like to name him Ephraim."

"Another Hebrew name?"

"Yes. It means 'double fruit.'"

"You want to call our son a fruit?"

"Asenath, when both you and he came through childbirth in such good shape, I got down on my knees and thanked God.

I realize that I've been unbelievably blessed to have such a wonderful wife and two healthy sons—not to mention all the material possessions like this house and chariots plus having a job I enjoy. God has truly blessed us and has made me fertile in the land of my affliction."

"If all of that is what 'double fruit' means to you, then Ephraim might be a good name for our son. At least it sounds a bit more positive than what you named our first boy."

"Manasseh? I thought you liked that name."

"I like the sound of it, but I had some reservations about the meaning. Let's face it: I never thought I'd call my first child a name meaning 'Making to forget.'"

"Ah, sweetheart, think of that as being a complement to you and God for blessing me so much that you have made me forget completely my hardships and my parental home."

"Personally, Joseph, I think Pharaoh made a very wise choice when he appointed you as his second in command."

"The bountiful harvests we have had these past six years have made it easier. But after this next year comes seven years of famine. We only confiscated one-fifth of the grain. Our farms will have to produce enough during the lean years to supplement what we've set aside in storage."

"Will it be enough?"

"I must trust in God to see us through. I'm following his directions."

Chapter 19

"I was told to report to you immediately, Sire," Joseph said while kneeling before Pharaoh.

"Yes, Joseph. We have had seven years of record-breaking harvests—just as you predicted. What happens now?"

"Now comes the famine. You have undoubtedly noticed the lack of rain."

"Yes, I have."

"During our years of plenty, I have had grain storage facilities built in each of our major cities to facilitate distribution to the people, although our major holding areas are nearer where the grain is grown. I plan to closely monitor the distribution. We have reassigned persons caught being dishonest over the past seven years so that I am reasonably confident that the people currently in charge of the production, harvesting, storage or distribution of grain are honest and reliable."

"I think I remember a few of the cases."

"Probably, my Lord. Depending upon the severity of the crime, some were reassigned to more menial positions, some became slaves, and some were executed."

Pharaoh rubbed his chin before leaning forward and asking, "What's the total amount of grain you have in storage?"

"I'm not sure. Because the total exceeds the mathematical terms available in the Egyptian language, I have found it more expedient to tally each of the storage facilities separately. But that also makes it easier for me to keep closer tabs on each place."

Chapter 20

When the seven years of abundance ended, the seven years of famine began, just as Joseph had said they would. At first there was sufficient grain on hand in the homes and markets of the land to meet the needs of the people. This famine, however, was more severe than those of prior years, and the normal reserves and resources of the people began to be depleted. As the Egyptians faced hunger and possible starvation, they cried out to Pharaoh for help.

Pharaoh said to his people, "Go to Joseph; whatever he tells you to do, you shall do."

Joseph oversaw the sale and distribution of grain to the people. Initially the people who came were Egyptians who purchased the grain using money earned during the years of plenty. As the famine dragged on and worsened, the Egyptian coins were gradually replaced with other possessions such as gold, silver, jewelry, and artistic artifacts. When they ran out of property that could be traded for food, hungry people pledged themselves to do labor for Pharaoh and the Egyptian government.

Since the famine extended beyond the borders of Egypt, foreigners began making their way to Joseph and his storehouses of grain.

One day Joseph was working with

some of his attendants when he heard some chatter from the long line of people seeking to buy grain—chatter that was both different and familiar. Since it was in a foreign tongue, it was different from almost all the words and expressions he had heard for the past twenty years. But the words, sounds and inflections were also familiar. Too familiar.

Joseph turned toward the chatter and soon found the speakers. His ten older brothers were standing in the line talking with each other.

He recognized them at once, of course. They were older, balder, not in as prime a physical condition, and it appeared they had been missing some meals—but that was to be expected in the midst of a famine. Benjamin wasn't with them. Had they mistreated him too?

Joseph dismissed his attendant, leaned forward in his throne-like chair and studied his brothers more closely. Their clothes were dusty and a bit ragged, and these herdsmen looked totally out of place in the marble buildings of sophisticated Egypt. They gaped at the palaces and temples around them in wide-eyed wonder and spoke in hushed phrases.

The brothers looked up at Joseph, but their eyes showed no recognition of him. No surprise there. The last time they had seen him he was a Hebrew teenager being led off by foreigners as a slave. The thirty-nine-year-old man on the throne in charge of distributing grain was an

Egyptian prince in royal robes and an Egyptian headdress and eye makeup.

They didn't even converse directly with the Egyptian prince, but rather communicated through an interpreter. They said they wished to purchase grain and poured out their pieces of silver on the table.

Joseph had named his first son Manasseh ["God has made me forget"], but the sight of his brothers with silver brought back painful memories. The last time he had seen silver in the hands of his brothers was when they had sold him to Ishmaelites for twenty pieces of the stuff. They had even seriously considered killing him or just letting him die in the pit.

Had they changed, or were they still the same as they had been two decades earlier? If they were jealous of him when he was just a kid, what would be their reactions now if they knew that the man in royal robes and wearing Pharaoh's signet ring was their little brother?

Seeing them bowing down before him also brought to mind certain childhood dreams. Was all of this part of God's plan and purpose? Joseph needed more time to think through this sudden development, pray about it, and determine what should be done. Pretending he did not recognize them, Joseph said through his interpreter, "Where do you come from?"

"From the land of Canaan to procure

food," they replied.

"I think you are spies. You have come to see how much the famine has weakened our land and exposed our nakedness."

When his words were interpreted to his brothers, they fell on their faces before him and said, "No, my lord! Truly your servants have come to procure food. We are all of us sons of the same man. We are honest hard-working men who have never been spies."

"No! You are spies."

"We your servants were twelve brothers, all sons of a certain man in the land of Canaan. Our youngest brother is home with our father, and one brother is no more."

"I still think you are spies, but I am willing to put you to the test. Unless your youngest brother comes here and verifies your story, by the life of Pharaoh you shall not depart this land. Let one of you go and bring your brother while the rest of you remain confined. This shall be the test to determine whether you are actually telling the truth."

Joseph then confined them in the guardhouse for three days. On the third day Joseph sent for them and told them, "I have decided to test your honesty by keeping one of you here in detention while the rest of you may go home with the grain you have purchased for your starving households — but you must bring me your youngest brother so that your words may be verified."

Speaking to one another in Hebrew, they said, "Alas, we are being punished because of what we did to our brother. We looked on at Joseph's anguish, yet we paid no heed as he pleaded with us. That is why this distress has come upon us."

Reuben shook his head and said, "Didn't I tell you not to hurt the boy or do any wrong to him? But you paid no attention to what I said and sold him while I was away. Now comes the reckoning for his blood."

They didn't know that the Egyptian prince who had spoken harshly to them understood everything they were saying to each other, for he had used an interpreter when conversing with them. But Joseph understood—and he turned away, quickly left the room, and wept.

When he had regained his composure, he returned and chose Simeon to be the one kept in Egypt. He had learned by listening to his brothers that Reuben, the first-born son, had tried to save him. Thus, he kept the second-born brother instead, having Simeon bound as the other brothers watched.

Then Joseph gave orders to fill their sacks with clean threshed grain, return each one's money to his personal sackcloth bag, and give them provisions for their journey. When this had been done, the brothers were sent on their way back to Canaan.

Chapter 21

When the brothers made camp the first night after leaving Egypt, they unloaded their donkeys and set up their tents. Judah opened his sack of grain to get feed for his donkey—and saw his money right there in the mouth of his bag.

"Oh my God!" he exclaimed. "My money has been returned. It's here in my bag!"

"What is this that God has done to us?" asked Reuben.

Dan turned to him and said, "Are you kidding? Judah came out ahead. He's got a full sack of grain, provisions for the journey, and still has all his money."

"No, Dan," said Reuben. "Just think this through. That Egyptian lord thinks we are spies. Judah still has his money as well as the grain and provisions. We're probably being framed to be considered either spies or criminals."

"Well," said Judah. "Whatever is happening is beyond our control."

Reuben shook his head. "I fear we are being punished for what we did to our brother Joseph."

All the brothers eyed each other nervously.

When they came to their father, Jacob, in the land of Canaan, they told him, "The man who is lord of Egypt spoke harshly to us and accused us of being spies. We said to him, 'We are honest men and have never been spies. There were twelve of us brothers, all sons of the same man—but one is no more and the youngest is now with our father in the land of Canaan.'

"The man who is lord of the land said to us, 'By this I shall know whether you are really honest men. Leave one of your brothers with me when you return to your starving households with grain. But when you come back here again you must bring your youngest brother to me so that I know you are telling the truth and are not spies. I will then return your brother to you, and you shall be free to go.'"

As they were emptying their sacks,

they discovered that each of their money bags had been returned to them in each man's sack of grain. The discovery both dismayed and frightened them, since they realized they had taken a large supply of grain from Egypt without paying for it.

Jacob wailed, "It is always me that you bereave. Joseph is no more and Simeon is no more, and now you would take away Benjamin. Why do all these disasters always happen to me?"

Reuben said to his father, "You may kill my two sons if I do not bring Benjamin back to you. Put him in my care and I will return him to you."

Jacob said, "Benjamin must not go down with you, for his brother is dead and he alone is left. If he meets with disaster on the journey to Egypt, you will send my white head down to Sheol in grief."

Chapter 22

Joseph quietly watched as his brothers' sacks of grain were loaded onto their donkeys and they began their journey back to Canaan. Then he turned and asked his chief steward, "Were all my orders carried out?"

"Yes, my lord. We filled all the bags of each of the Canaanite men with clean threshed grain, we placed each of their bags of silver into their personal sacks, and we provided them with provisions for their journey back to Canaan."

"Very good. You have done well. Place the prisoner in the jail where we keep Pharaoh's prisoners. Make certain that he is well cared for, but don't provide him with an interpreter."

That night Joseph appeared to be lost in thought as he ate his evening meal and interacted with his wife and children. He retired earlier than usual to his study, where he gazed at nothing in particular while sitting in his favorite chair.

His reverie was interrupted by his wife, who asked him, "What's wrong, Joseph?"

"What do you mean?"

"For the last several days you haven't acted like yourself. You've hardly talked to me and the boys. You spend an abnormal amount of time by yourself just staring into space. You can't seem to decide whether you're happy, sad, serene or agitated. You have more mood changes than even what I sometimes go through—and I've heard you complain about mine."

"Oh, it's nothing."

"I know better than that, Joseph. I'm your wife. I need to know what's bothering you."

Joseph sighed, rubbed his chin, and then sighed again. "Yeah, Asenath, you're right. Do you recall what I told you about how I ended up in Egypt?"

"Yes. You said a gang of men had kidnapped you in Canaan and sold you to a caravan of foreigners—it seems like you called them Ishmaelites—who were headed for Egypt, where you were sold as a slave."

"That's right. Well, three days ago that same gang of men showed up here trying to buy grain."

"Whoa! Did you have them arrested?"

"Yes, but not for what they did to me. Instead, I accused them of being spies."

"Are they spies?"

"No, but that allowed me to jail them without letting them know I was the same person they had sold into slavery. Well, today I let all but one of them out of jail and allowed them to go back to their home with the grain they needed."

"I don't understand. Why did you do that?"

"It just seemed like the right thing to do. I guess I may want to know if they are still the same as they were or if they changed. They didn't know I could understand everything they said to each other."

"What did they say?"

"They claimed they are all sons of the same man and that they have another brother—the youngest one—who is back home in Canaan with their father. I told them that in order to get their brother out of jail they must bring the youngest brother to me so that I know they are actually telling the truth."

"But you already said they're not spies, which indicates you know they're not lying."

"Oh, I know they're telling the truth—but I desperately want to see their youngest brother."

"Why?"

"Because he's Benjamin, my youngest brother."

"Oh." Asenath caught her breath and her eyes widened as realization set in. "Oooohh."

She took several breaths before continuing. "That means you were sold out by your own brothers. Oh—that's disgusting, that's horrible, that's unspeakable, that's . . . that's . . .

"Oh, my dear, dearest Joseph. No wonder you've been so preoccupied. To be betrayed by your own family. Sold out by the ones who should be your protectors. I can't think of anything more . . . more—"

Asenath's words failed her and she left the sentence hanging. Instead, she reached out to her husband, embraced him, and they both just let go and cried.

Chapter 23

Several months later Joseph was walking past the garden adjacent to his house when he caught sight of his wife sitting on the ground with her back to him. At first he thought she might be gardening, since she was next to some of her favorite flowers. But Asenath wasn't watering them or otherwise tending to them.

As Joseph quietly walked closer, he noted she wasn't even looking at the flowers. She had her eyes closed and appeared to be in deep meditation. He moved beside Asenath and stood watching her for several minutes before she became aware of his presence.

"Oh!" she said. "You startled me."

"What are you doing?"

"Praying."

"Praying? Out here in the garden?"

"This is where I come when I pray to your God."

"Why here?"

"I feel more comfortable praying to my husband's Canaanite God when I'm in my own little bit of Canaan."

Joseph looked at her without comprehending what she meant for a moment. Then he smiled, nodded and said, "Ah, yes. You mean these flowers you had imported from Canaan."

"That's part of it. I also had Omron bring back a wagon load of soil. I used part of it for planting these pretty Canaanite flowers I had him bring me, but most of it is here where I kneel while praying to your God."

"Since God created everything, he doesn't need you to be on particular soil in order to communicate with him."

"I know . . . You've told me that before. But please be patient with your foolish wife as I struggle to work with new concepts after spending a lifetime thinking of each nation as having its own peculiar gods.

"Remember my background, Joseph. My father is chief priest for the Egyptian sun god, Ra, and even my name means 'belonging to the Egyptian goddess Neith.' I grew up worshiping the various Egyptian gods and goddesses. I had never even considered there could be only one single God who created everything until Pharaoh gave me to you in marriage.

"I have prayed to the various Egyptian gods and goddesses more times than I can count—but I have never had a single one of my prayers answered by any of them. Not one! Then you interpreted dreams that none of Pharaoh's counselors, wise men, soothsayers or priests—including my own father—could interpret. I watched carefully to see if the interpretation you said came from your God was true. The seven years of plenty produced crops beyond any we've previously experienced. Then they ended and we have had two years of famine and will soon head into our third year. I have no doubt that the famine will continue just as you predicted.

"It's obvious to me that your God knows the future and that he may even fully control it. It's also obvious to me that you have a personal relationship with him—and that's something I desperately desire to have as well. So I've been slipping out of the house and coming here to pray as often as I can.

"It may not be necessary to come to this spot, but I feel more comfortable doing it this way. Please don't scold me,

Joseph, or forbid me from seeking your God."

"Oh Asenath, Asenath: I love you. Of course you can pray to God whenever and wherever you wish. But tell me, why are you seeking God? Is there a problem you have that we need to discuss? Can I help you in any way?"

Asenath hesitated before looking into Joseph's eyes and smiling. "Yes, Joseph, there is a problem, but it is your problem rather than mine—and I have been seeking wisdom from your God so that I might be able to help you with it."

"My problem? What do you mean?"

"I've watched the internal conflict going on inside you as you try to decide what to do about your brothers who betrayed you. You know the famine is only getting worse and that it will continue to do so. That means they would have to be back to see you even if you hadn't kept one of them hostage.

"You've already told me that you're longing to see your youngest brother again. I think this entire matter is eating at you and occupying your attention. Am I right?"

"Yes, you're right. I've got to see Benjamin and make certain he hasn't been mistreated the way they mistreated me. Also, he's my only full brother — the only one who was born to my mother. If the others have been cruel to him, then that means they haven't changed and I'll be more likely to give them the justice they deserve."

"A chance for revenge?"

"Maybe."

"What happened to the part about God making you forget all your troubles and all your father's household?"

Joseph shot a hard look at his wife before answering. "I thought my old wounds had healed—but seeing my brothers again has pulled off the scabs and opened those wounds. Why did they have to show up? I was content to let bygones be bygones."

"Yes, Joseph, you were content to let your past remain in your past. But maybe your God wasn't."

"What do you mean?"

"The names you gave our boys indicate you had not truly forgotten your past. It was still seething and festering under the surface. Maybe your God thought it was time for you to confront it and bring it out into the open."

"And then what?"

"I don't know. Maybe you'll decide now is your chance for revenge . . . justice . . . retribution. Or you might decide to leave that to your God. Now might be the time for mercy, cleansing, and restoration. It's your decision, but the rest of your life—and theirs—and your relationship with your family hangs on what you decide. In any event, it's an important enough decision that I've been bathing it in prayer—and I strongly suspect you have been as well."

"As usual, your suspicions are correct, Asenath."

Chapter 24

Since the severity of the famine did not diminish, Jacob's household consumed the rations his sons had brought from Egypt. Jacob told his boys, "Go again to Egypt and procure more food for us."

"Only if you let Benjamin go with us," said Judah. "The Egyptian lord warned us, 'Don't let me see your faces again unless your youngest brother is with you.'"

"Why did you serve me so ill as to tell that man that you had another brother?"

"Because he kept asking about us and our family, saying, 'Is your father still living? Do you have another brother?' We merely answered his questions. How were we to know he would demand that we bring our youngest brother to prove we were telling the truth and were not spies?"

Judah started to turn away but then turned back and said, "Send Benjamin in my care. I myself will be surety for him and you may hold me responsible. If I do not bring him back to you and set him before you, I shall stand guilty before you forever.

"Only let us be on our way, for we could have been there and back twice if we had not dawdled so long with your moaning and needless arguments. Just remember that we will all die if we don't get more food."

Jacob groaned and leaned forward in his chair, holding his head in his hands. He sighed and said, "If it must be so, then do this: Take some of the choice products of the land in your baggage and carry them down as a gift for the man. Egypt has bee's honey but imports grape honey from Canaan, so take him some of that. Also take some balm, gum, ladanum, almonds, and pistachio nuts. And take with you double the money, carrying back with you the money that was replaced in the mouths of your bags. Perhaps it was a mistake."

Again Jacob sighed. "Take your brother too and go back at once to the man. And may El Shaddai dispose the man to show you mercy, release and return your other brother as well as Benjamin. As for me, if I am to be bereaved, I shall be bereaved."

Thus Benjamin joined his older brothers as they made their way back to Egypt.

Chapter 25

When Joseph saw Benjamin with his older brothers, he gazed intently at his younger brother for several minutes. *So Benjamin is still alive and well. He's looking good; I can't tell if he's been mistreated, but I can check it out more closely.*

Joseph called the servant who was over his household to his side and told him to take the eleven Hebrew men to his house, slaughter and prepare an animal, and prepare a meal for the Canaanite men, for they were to dine with him at noon. He then had his Hebrew interpreter take the brothers to Joseph's home. Since none of Joseph's plans were explained to his brothers, they were alarmed and frightened when they were taken there.

"Why have we been brought here?" asked Levi.

"I don't know," said Reuben. "Perhaps it's a trap."

Judah looked around nervously before answering. "It must be because of the money replaced in our bags the first time that we have been brought inside, as a pretext to attack us and seize us as slaves along with our pack animals."

Seeing the interpreter standing with the house steward at the entrance to the house, Judah walked up to them and said, "If you please, my lord, we came down once before to procure food. But when we camped that night and opened our bags, there was each one's money in the mouth of his bag. Our money had been returned to us in full. So we have brought it back with us along with more money to purchase more food. We do not know who put the money into our bags."

When Judah's words were translated for the steward, he replied, "All is well with you. Don't be afraid, for we received your payment. Perhaps your God may have restored your money to you."

Simeon was released from jail and allowed to join his brothers. Their donkeys were watered and fed, and the brothers were given water so they could wash their feet. When they were informed that Joseph would be joining them at noon for lunch, they laid out their gifts while waiting for him.

When Joseph came home, all eleven of his brothers bowed low to the ground before him and presented their gifts for him.

Speaking through an interpreter, Joseph greeted them by asking, "How is your aged father of whom you spoke? Is he still in good health?"

They replied, "It is well with your servant our father; he is still in good health." Again they bowed, made obeisance, and wished him *shalom* ("peace") several times.

Joseph motioned at Benjamin and asked, "Is this your youngest brother of whom you spoke to me? May God be gracious to you, my son."

Joseph immediately turned and rushed from the room, for he was about to be overcome with tears. After weeping in private, he washed his face, regained his composure, and ordered that the noon meal be served.

Three separate tables were set up. The eleven Hebrew brothers ate at one table, the Egyptians ate at another, and Joseph ate by himself at a table on a slightly raised dais positioned near the other two tables. When the brothers were seated, they noticed they were seated in order of birth from the firstborn to the youngest.

Reuben turned to Simeon and asked, "How do they know our relative ages to seat us in this order?"

Simeon shook his head and gestured that he didn't know.

When the waiters brought the brothers their food, they gave Benjamin preferential treatment and more food than any of his older brothers.

Joseph quietly watched their reactions to see if his brothers exhibited the same spirit of jealousy they had shown toward him many years earlier. Although they appeared to notice the inequality, they did not seem to be upset by it.

The brothers paid for the grain they were purchasing and were given lodging while their donkeys were packed so they could leave for Canaan early the next morning.

Chapter 26

When Joseph retired to his bedroom that night, he was greeted by his wife, "I saw that you ate the noon meal with your brothers."

"Yes, Asenath, it was good to see them again."

"Did you let them know you're their long-lost brother?"

"Not yet. I never spoke Hebrew or let them know I could understand their language."

"But you listened."

"Yes, I listened—and observed. And let my emotions fight within me."

"I suspected as much. What have you learned so far?"

"I had our servants show favoritism to Benjamin, but I couldn't tell that it bothered the others. However, they'll get a much stronger test tomorrow."

"Tomorrow? But aren't they heading back home to Canaan tomorrow?"

"They are. Their bags are loaded and their animals are packed. But I had my chief steward hide my personal silver cup in Benjamin's bag."

"Benjamin? But I thought he was your favorite brother."

"Benjamin is my only full brother.

Mother died while giving birth to him."

"Then why would you accuse him of stealing your cup?"

"I want to know if my older brothers will abandon him and sell him out like they did me."

Asenath nodded her head, smiled, and replied, "As you said: It's a much stronger test as to whether they have changed and repented for what they did to you."

Chapter 27

With the first light of morning, the eleven brothers set off for Canaan with their pack animals. They had just left the city when Joseph's chief steward and a detachment of soldiers overtook them.

Speaking through a translator, the steward said, "Why did you repay good with evil? Why have you stolen that which my master uses for divination and foretelling the future? It is a wicked thing that you have done."

Judah protested, "Why does my lord say such things? Far be it from your servants to do anything of the kind! We even brought back all the money we had found in our bags the first time — brought it all the way back from Canaan. Doesn't that show that we are honest men? How then could we have stolen anything from your master's house?"

"That's right," said Reuben. "Look through our things. If you find anything that's been stolen from your master, whoever's bag it is in shall die — and the rest of us will be your slaves."

The steward shook his head and said, "Although what you are proposing is right, only the one with whom it is found shall be my master's slave. The rest of you may go free."

Each of Jacob's sons lowered his bag to the ground and the steward searched each sack, beginning with the oldest brother's bag and continuing until the silver cup was discovered in Benjamin's personal sack.

Instead of allowing Benjamin to be taken while the others fled, the brothers all tore their clothes in anguish, reloaded their donkeys, and returned to the city. When they arrived at Joseph's house, they prostrated themselves in front of him.

Joseph pretended to be shocked and angry. "What is this deed that you have done? Didn't you realize that a man like me practices divination?"

Judah replied, "What can we say to our lord? How can we plead? How can we prove our innocence? God has uncovered the crime we have apparently committed. Here we are, then, slaves of you, our lord — the rest of us just as much as he in whose possession the goblet was found."

"No," said Joseph. "Far be it from me to act that way. Only the man in whose possession the goblet was found shall be my slave. The rest of you may go back in peace to your father."

Judah rose, moved toward Joseph, and again kneeled in submission. "Please, my lord, let your servant appeal to you, though you be equal to Pharaoh. Please let me speak and do not be impatient with what I must say. When you asked us if we had another brother or a father, we told you that we have an old father and a brother who was the child of his old age. He is the only son still living who was born to our father's favorite wife so that our father dotes on him.

"You said to us, your servants, 'Bring the boy down to me that I may see him.' We told you, 'The boy cannot leave his father, for our father would die if he were taken from him.' But you said, 'Do not let me see your faces again unless you bring your youngest brother with you.' We repeated your words to our father and told him we could not return to you unless we brought our youngest brother with us.

"Our father said to us, 'As you know, my wife bore me two sons. But one is gone from me—torn by a beast—and I have not seen him since. If you take this one from me too and he meets with disaster, you will send my white head down to Sheol in sorrow.' Now if we come to our father and the boy is not with us—since his own life is so bound up with his—when he sees that the boy is not with us, he will die. We will have sent the white head of our father down to Sheol in grief.

"Your servant has pledged himself for the boy to my father, saying, 'If I do not bring him back to you, I shall stand guilty before my father forever.' Therefore, please let your servant remain as a slave to my lord instead of the boy. I offer myself as your slave for life in place of my youngest brother. Only let the boy go back with his brothers to our father, for how can we go back to our father unless the boy is with us? Please don't make me witness the woe that would overtake my father if his youngest son does not return to him."

Chapter 28

Joseph could no longer control himself or his emotions before all his attendants. He cried out, "Have everyone withdraw from me!"

The interpreter asked, "Do you want me to go as well, or should I stay to help interpret the words of these Hebrew shepherds?"

"Go!" Joseph ordered in Egyptian.

When all his attendants had left so that Joseph was alone with his brothers, Joseph turned toward them, his eyes full of tears, and cried out in Hebrew, "I am Joseph, your brother. Is my father still well?"

All eleven brothers stood mute in shocked silence. Nine of them had watched him be led away as a seventeen-year-old kid into a life of slavery. Most slaves had a rather short life expectancy, even more so if they were foreigners in a strange land with different language and customs. How could their bratty kid brother have risen to be the powerful ruler now standing before them?

It had been twenty-two years since Joseph had vanished from their sight. There had been no contact or communication between them during all that time other than the rather strained words exchanged while the Hebrew men attempted to buy grain from the Egyptians—and those words had been with the assistance of a translator.

Yet the powerful Egyptian official was apparently their long-lost (and presumably dead) brother—just as he claimed to be. It was shocking. It was unbelievable. It didn't make sense—but then again, maybe it did. It would explain how their birth order was known. It would explain how their money got back into their bags. It would even explain what the meanings were for those infernal dreams their kid brother bragged about that made the others so mad all those years ago.

The brothers came out of their shocked trance when they heard Joseph say, "Come forward to me." When they came forward, he said, "I am your brother Joseph, he whom you sold into Egyptian slavery. Do not be distressed or reproach yourselves because you sold me hither; it was to save many lives that God sent me ahead of you.

"It is now two years that there has been famine in the land, and there are still five more years to come in which there shall be insufficient yield from tilling. God sent me ahead of you to ensure your survival and to save your lives in an extraordinary deliverance.

"So don't blame yourselves for sending me here as a slave. Rather, it was

God who arranged for it to be done. God made me as a father to Pharaoh, lord of all his household, and ruler over the whole land of Egypt.

"Now hurry back to my father and say to him, 'Your son Joseph is alive and is lord and ruler over all of Egypt. Joseph wants you to join him in Egypt without delay. You will dwell in the region of Goshen, where you will be near to Joseph—you, your children and grandchildren, your flocks and herds, and all that is yours. There I will provide for you, for there are yet five years of famine to come.'"

Joseph reached out, embraced his brothers, and said, "Return to our father and tell him everything—and then bring him and your families and herds here as quickly as you can."

Joseph kissed all his brothers and wept with them, but he showed special attention to Benjamin. The two sons of Rachel held each other close and cried tears of joy.

Chapter 29

When word reached Pharaoh that Joseph's brothers had come, the king and his courtiers were pleased. Pharaoh said to Joseph, "Say to your brothers, 'Load up your beasts and go at once to your home in Canaan. Get your father and your households and come back here to me. I will give you the best of the land of Egypt. I want to show you the gratitude we have for your brother and how he saved our lives and our land. Don't worry about leaving some of your belongings in Canaan, for the best of Egypt shall be yours."

Joseph did as Pharaoh had commanded, giving his brothers new clothing as well as wagon loads of provisions for their journey. He also sent ten male donkeys loaded with the best things of Egypt, and ten female donkeys laden with grain, bread and provisions for their return trip.

As he sent his brothers off on their way, he told them, "Don't quarrel or get angry on your journey, don't be afraid, and hurry back with the rest of your families and possessions."

When the brothers had passed from his sight, Joseph returned home, where Asenath greeted him by asking, "How was the family reunion?"

"It went well. In other words, my brothers passed their tests with flying colors."

"Tell me about it."

"I gave them every opportunity to abandon Benjamin and save themselves—but they didn't do it. Instead, Judah offered to become my personal slave for life if only I would let Benjamin go back home to his father. Judah was the same one who hatched the plan to sell me into slavery with the Ishmaelites. My brothers have changed so that I really believe we can be a family once again."

"How did your brothers react to discovering you were their next of kin?

"Shock. Disbelief. Then fear for what I might do. Finally—relief, acceptance and joy."

"And what are your feelings about it all?

"I'm glad it worked out the way it did. It's kind of funny. When I was first sold into slavery, I wanted my brothers to pay for what they'd done. I thought of it as being justice, but it was probably more a desire for revenge and to get even with them. They had robbed me of my home, and I had been especially close to Dad and Benjamin. I wanted to see them again and be close to them but couldn't while I was a slave or in prison.

"Then when I was placed in charge of Egypt, I decided to let bygones be bygones. I had been gone thirteen years, didn't know whether they were still alive or what they had told our father about my disappearance. Maybe things would be better if I just left things as they were. I thanked God, Pharaoh, and you for my new life and position—and was content to leave my past in the past and just move on."

"You were, but apparently your God wasn't."

Joseph gave her a hard look. Asenath just smiled knowingly.

"I think you're right, Asenath. God caused it to happen—but why? You act as if you know why he didn't let me leave my past in the past."

"No, I merely have an idea why; an observation."

"All right. What's your observation?"

"This famine is like none other we have ever experienced. It's a famine of supernatural proportions that would have wrecked our economy, killed our people, and destroyed Egypt. Yet you handled it without breaking a sweat. You were also able to navigate the journey from being a lowly slave to becoming ruler of Egypt without letting it go to your head. You're a good and loving husband to me and are a great father to our boys. The only thing that I've seen knock you for a loop is encountering your brothers after all these years. Betrayal by loved ones will do that. You may have been content to let bygones be bygones and cut all ties to your past—but your God wasn't. Why, Joseph? Why did God bring them back into your life?"

"You've obviously been thinking about this, Asenath—so tell me what you've come up with."

"Relationships matter to your God. That's one of the major differences between your God and the gods I've worshiped all my life. You have a personal relationship with your God that's real. Because relationships matter to him, restoration of broken relationships is also important to him. So God made it possible for your relationship with your family to be repaired and restored."

"Oh, I hope so, Asenath. I certainly hope so. I've longed for reunion and restoration all these years but didn't know how to accomplish it."

Asenath looked intently into Joseph's eyes and smiled. "I'm so glad you have a God who cares about such things—cares enough to cause it to happen."

Chapter 30

When Jacob's sons returned home to their father in Canaan, he came out to meet them. He mutely stood in the doorway staring at the sight before him, but was unable to comprehend what he saw.

"What's all this?" he asked while looking toward the twenty extra donkeys in the boys' caravan.

"Great news, father!" shouted Judah exuberantly. "Our brother Joseph is still alive, and he is the ruler over the whole land of Egypt."

Jacob staggered backward, shaking his head and moaning, "I'm too old and frail for you to play cruel tricks or games with me. Now you're talking nonsense."

"No, really father. Joseph is alive!"

"It can't be. He was killed by some animal. You yourself brought me his blood-soaked tunic twenty-something years ago. Now you want me to believe he's still alive?"

"It's true, father. Look at all the good things of Egypt he has sent to you as gifts."

"Oh my: Wagons, donkeys, grain, new clothes. Can it really be true?"

Jacob wandered through the caravan of goods accompanying his sons, gazed in wonder at all he saw, and then turned to Benjamin for confirmation. "Tell me, my boy, is it true? Does your brother actually live?"

"Yes, father. It's true. We have been to his house, we have eaten with him, and I have held him in my arms and kissed him. He's alive, well, and is ruler of Egypt. Furthermore, he wants all of us to come and live in Egypt with him."

"But Egypt is a foreign land with foreign gods who are pagan. I am now an old man who is getting more feeble all the time. Is it safe for us to go there?"

"Oh father, think: Joseph—your son and my brother—rules Egypt and will protect us. We have thought him dead all these years—but he's alive, he's well, and he wants us to join him there."

"Enough! My son Joseph is still alive! I must go and see him before I die."

Chapter 31

Jacob gathered his children and their families and possessions, and they began the journey to Egypt. When they came to Beer-sheba, he offered sacrifices to the God of his father Isaac. That night God called, "Jacob! Jacob!" to him in a vision. "I am God—the God of your father. Do not be afraid of going to Egypt, for that is where I will make your descendants into a great nation. I Myself will go down with you to Egypt, and I Myself will also bring you back, and Joseph's hand shall close your eyes."

When Jacob awoke, he set out from Beer-sheba for Egypt. His sons put him and their wives and children into the wagons that Pharaoh had sent to transport them. They took their livestock and the wealth they had amassed in the land of Canaan.

As they neared Egypt, Judah was sent ahead of the caravan to contact Joseph and to point the way to Goshen, where they had been told they would be living. Joseph rode to Goshen in his chariot to meet his father, brothers and their families. Jacob and Joseph embraced each other and wept unashamedly for quite a while until the tears no longer would come.

Jacob looked into Joseph's eyes, smiled and said, "Now that I have seen for myself that you are still alive, I can die with contentment and satisfaction."

Epilogue

Jacob lived in Egypt with Joseph for the last seventeen years of his life—which formed a sort of bookend for the first seventeen years of Joseph's life when he lived in Canaan with his father and brothers. In between those seventeen-year periods were the years when Joseph faced some of the stiffest challenges and worst obstacles life has to offer—betrayal by friends or loved ones, slavery, economic bankruptcy, being unjustly accused of immoral activity and criminal acts, imprisonment, and abandonment—but he met each challenge and overcame the obstacles, becoming the man God could use to save many lives, change the course of history, and serve as an inspiring role model for countless people through the ages.

If you enjoyed
Joseph's Quest, read on for a preview of

Saul's Quest

A historical fiction novel
About Saul of Tarsus
(who later became the apostle Paul)

by Bill Kincaid

Ananias awakened from a troubled sleep. Nightmares generally fade quickly from memory as conscious thoughts replace the ethereal wisps of subconscious dreams—but this one was different. It had been especially vivid, and still burned in his memory like a festering sore.

In his dream, Ananias and a friend were being chased by a band of men. Ananias' friend tripped, fell, and was quickly surrounded by their pursuers. When he tried to get up, they knocked him back down, tied his hands, and took him prisoner. Then the ruffians continued chasing Ananias. No matter where he turned, Ananias' path was blocked by men who were either chasing him or who were dragging away other friends as prisoners.

Dreams are strange things. Sometimes you *know* something without being aware of precisely how or why you know it. In this case, Ananias somehow knew that the men chasing them had been sent by Jewish religious authorities and that capture meant almost certain torture or death.

For months, the high priest and his henchmen had been rounding up followers of Jesus of Nazareth and putting them into jail. Several of Ananias' friends had been beaten or flogged with whips, and at least one of them had been stoned to death.

In his nightmare, Ananias could barely run fast enough to elude his pursuers. He woke with a start when his wife shook him.

Ananias looked around frantically. His running legs had kicked the cover off his bed, and he was breathing hard and covered with sweat.

"What happened?" she asked worriedly.

"I dreamed the persecutors of the church in Jerusalem were coming after us to drag us back to the high priest and the council. It was awful."

"It was just a bad dream. Calm down."

"But it was so real. So vivid. I could even recognize our friends . . . and some of the ones who were persecuting us."

"Just relax and compose yourself. I'll get us something to eat."

"Very well, Rachel," he replied as he sat back and looked around him. With the exception of the displaced covers on his bed, all appeared to be normal. The chairs and table were still in their proper place, the gray and brown stones forming the walls of his room looked familiar and comforting, and no ruffians appeared to be lurking anywhere.

After composing himself for a few minutes, Ananias rose and walked to a wash basin. He poured some water from a pitcher into the basin and washed his face. He then slipped a *me'il* cloak over his undergarment and sat back down to consider the nightmare he had experienced.

Suddenly he felt as if he was surrounded by a bright light that obscured everything else.

"Ananias," called a voice out of the light.

"Yes, Lord?" he answered.

"There is something I want you to do."

"What is it, Lord?"

The bright light dissipated, and Ananias saw a man kneeling down before him, deeply engaged in prayer.

"I want you to go to the house of Judas on Straight Street."

"Is that the wealthy merchant named Judas?"

"Yes, that's the one. Ask for a man from Tarsus named Saul, for he is praying," the voice continued. "In a vision he has seen a man named Ananias come and place his hands on him to restore his sight."

The man kneeling in prayer in Ananias' vision raised his head and looked at Ananias. It was the leader of the ruffians who had disrupted his sleep in his nightmare!

"Lord!" exclaimed Ananias. "I have heard many reports about this man and all the harm he has done to your saints in Jerusalem. Now he has come here with authority from the chief priests to arrest all who call upon your name."

"Ananias, trust me. Go do what I tell you to do. This man is my chosen instrument to carry my name before the Gentiles and their kings and before the people of Israel."

"But, Lord. He'll kill me. Many of your followers have suffered immensely because of this man."

"I will show him how much he must suffer for my name—but I need you to trust in me and do what I have asked you to do."

"Yes, Lord," Ananias answered, and the vision faded from his sight.

Ananias took several deep breaths before standing and looking around the room. He realized he would be walking into a den of his enemies. Yet he was supposed to lay his hands on the most dangerous man he could think of and help restore that man's sight. His body was wracked with an involuntary shudder at the thought.

"Is something wrong?" Rachel's question shook him out of his stupor.

"I'm not sure."

"Why? What happened?"

"The Lord just gave me a task I'd rather not do." Another spasm shook his body.

"What's the assignment?"

"I am to go down to the other end of our street and help restore the sight of Saul of Tarsus."

"Saul of Tarsus?"

"Yes."

"Are you sure?"

"I'm afraid so."

"That's crazy. Isn't he the one who has been leading the persecution of the church in Jerusalem?"

"That's the one."

"That can't be right. You just got through dreaming about those awful men coming after us to drag us back to Jerusalem. Then you wake up and suddenly decide you are going to make it easy for them. You'll just walk into their house and give yourself up. Is that what you're saying?"

"Not exactly. God didn't ask me to give myself up. He just wants me to lay hands on Saul and help restore his sight."

"Oh, that's *really* an improvement! Saul can't persecute you effectively now because he has been blinded. But you are going to restore his sight so he can more easily arrest you? Are you out of your mind?"

"The Lord told me that Saul was his chosen instrument for spreading the gospel."

"He's really helped spread it, all right. Because of his persecution, believers have fled Jerusalem and have scattered across the

Roman world. What will our friends think when they find out it was you who helped this awful man get back his sight so that he could continue persecuting the church?"

"I saw Saul in my vision. He was very earnestly praying."

"So what? After all, he is a Pharisee; they are always praying."

"No, you don't understand. He wasn't merely reciting a prayer; he was earnestly praying to the Lord. It was as if his world had been turned upside down, and he was asking God to reveal His will. The Lord said Saul had also received a vision. His vision was that I would be coming to him, laying my hands on him, and helping restore his sight."

Rachel suddenly broke down sobbing, "I don't want to lose you."

Ananias held her tightly in his arms and kissed her. "I love you, too."

"Don't go."

"I have to. We just have to trust the Lord in this."

"How do you know it was actually the Lord? Maybe it was just a continuation of your nightmare."

"No, this was different. I don't know how I'm sure it was the Lord. I just *know* it was."

"I still don't want you to go." She sighed and then added, "Please be careful."

"If you are worried about my safety, you can pray for me—and for Saul."

"I will. I love you. May God be with you."

"Thank you," Ananias smiled, and stepped out into the street.

Straight Street[1] was just that: a street that stretched out in a rather straight east-to-west line across Damascus. Ananias' house was near the eastern end of the street. In fact, from where he stood in front of his house, he could see the triple arches of the Roman Gate of the Sun, also known as the Eastern Gate. The large central arch was designed for horse-drawn vehicles, and was flanked by smaller arches for pedestrians.

Ananias breathed a quick prayer asking for the Lord's guidance and protection. Then he turned and headed west along a colonnade. An identical colonnade ran along the opposite side of the street. He passed various small shops, momentarily pausing as he realized that he might never see those familiar shops again. Nevertheless, since he

---

[1] Or Via Recta.

had committed himself to being God's instrument, he pressed on.

About seven hundred meters west of the Eastern Gate, Straight Street intersected the Cardo Maximus, the primary north-south road in Damascus. Ananias walked under a large Roman arch that spanned the intersection, and then paused as he looked up and down both streets.

He and Rachel had lived all their lives in the city of Damascus. They were devout Jews who believed that Jesus was the Messiah promised by God and prophesized by various Jewish prophets over the preceding centuries. It was their custom to worship in the local Jewish synagogue each Sabbath, and to join their friends who also believed in Jesus the following day, which they called the Lord's day. That belief had caused them to be targeted for persecution.

Ananias continued west about another three hundred meters down Straight Street, pausing in front of the large house belonging to Judas, a well-known local merchant. This is where his vision had directed him to come.

Ananias hesitated before knocking. He looked down and thought wryly to himself, *My knees are already knocking.* He again said a prayer for protection—this one somewhat longer than those before it—and knocked on the door.

No answer.

Good, he thought, and was tempted to leave.

He knocked again. A servant girl opened the door.

"Is Saul of Tarsus here?" he asked.

"Yes, sir."

"It is imperative that I see him immediately."

The girl nodded her head and said, "Follow me."

She led Ananias to a nearby room. On a mat in the center of the room sat a man deeply engaged in prayer. The scene was just as it had appeared in Ananias' vision. He froze as he looked at the man on the mat, realizing that Saul had come to Damascus for the express purpose of arresting and carrying away Ananias, Rachel and their friends. *As long as he is blinded, he may not be as much of a threat. But the Lord wants me to help him.* Ananias felt as if his heart were in his throat, his breath was labored, and he felt faint.

At any moment Saul's band of ruffians could seize him and carry him away. Ananias gulped, took a deep breath, and walked toward the man who haunted his sleep—the focal point of his nightmares.

If you enjoyed
Joseph's Quest, read on for a preview of

Wizard's Gambit

A science fiction / fantasy novel
by Bill Kincaid

Jackzen awakened from a sound sleep when his wife clutched his arm and fearfully asked, "What was that?"

"What's what?" His voice was groggy, but his muscles tensed.

They both listened intently for a moment, clutching each other in the predawn darkness.

"That!" Annika responded as a crash from the front room was quickly followed by the sound of loud footsteps rushing toward their bedroom, accompanied by the light of four burning torches.

Jackzen tossed aside the covers and started to spring from the bed, but was immediately forced back by a spear that cut him in his chest. He dropped onto the bed, clutching the top bedspread to his chest to stanch the bleeding. Only then did he look at the men surrounding him.

Soldiers. Or enforcers. Armed, surly, and mean.

"What's the meaning of this outrage?" he demanded.

"We're here to collect what you owe the Crown," responded one of them, a tall burly man standing to the right of the one who held the spear that had wounded him.

"We've already paid everything we owe the king," Jackzen protested. "All taxes and fees that were due, plus the extra assessments that enforcers demanded."

"That's what you claim," the enforcer who was apparently in charge replied. "We say you haven't paid what you owe."

"Kratzl!" Jackzen swore. "I can prove I paid it."

"Let's see your proof."

"Let me get up, and I'll get my receipt."

The officer motioned for his men to allow Jackzen to rise from the bed. Still holding the bedspread against his chest, Jackzen made his way to his dresser, rummaged through a drawer, and withdrew the vital document. He handed it to the officer triumphantly.

The officer read it carefully by the light of one of the torches, and then burned it in the fire.

"What other proof do you have to offer?"

"Hey!" Jackzen objected. "You can't do that!"

"I just did. What other proof do you have?"

"I shouldn't need any other proof. That receipt showed I paid all charges in full."

"Receipt? I don't see any receipt." The officer turned to his men. "Do any of you see a receipt?"

They laughed, sneered, and shook their heads.

"What proof do you now have to offer?"

Jackzen sputtered but held his tongue. "What is it you want?" he asked.

"I want your teenage daughter."

"Marza? Why?"

"Come off it, Jackzen. You're smarter than that. You know why."

"No! You have no right!" Jackzen yelled while lunging at the officer before being clubbed over the head by another enforcer.

"We have all the rights," Jackzen heard as he slipped from consciousness. "We're the king's enforcers."

About the Author

Although Bill Kincaid spent over 40 years practicing law in Texas, he started out as a writer and journalist. He was sports editor and political editor for his high school paper, editor of his university newspaper, and worked for several Texas newspapers before earning his Doctor of Jurisprudence degree from Texas Tech University's School of Law. Several of his articles and columns received state-wide honors.

Now that Kincaid is slowing down his legal practice, he finally has time to return to his writing roots, publishing two books in 2013 that are almost as different from each other as day is from night.

Nicodemus' Quest is a Christian historical fiction novel that makes as much use of Kincaid's ability to do detailed research as it does of his ability to tell a good story. *The Baptist Standard* called the book "a compelling, inventive, moving novel . . . a great story" and said that "extensive biblical, historical, geographical, archeological, and linguistic research exudes from each page."

On the other hand, *Ronald Raygun and the Sweeping Beauty* is a fractured fairy tale that satirizes such well known stories as *Sleeping Beauty*, *The Princess and the Pea*, and *Cinderella*. What makes the story even more fun is the humor that is woven throughout, not to mention various political references that permeate the work. Some are obvious (such as in the title), but most are extremely subtle and unobtrusive.

Kincaid is continuing to write on varied topics. In 2014, he published *Saul's Quest*, a novel about the Apostle Paul's life through his first missionary journey (while he was still known by his Hebrew name of Saul). *Wizard's Gambit* and *Kings & Vagabonds* are the first books in the Ventryvian Legacy series of science fiction fantasy novels.

He and his wife, Audette, have been married for more than fifty years and have three adult children, Cheryl-Annette, Christina, and Sharlene.